WIND RIDER

WIND RIDER

SUSAN WILLIAMS

Laura Geringer Books
An *Imprint of* HarperCollins*Publishers*

Wind Rider

 For information address
HarperCollins Children's Books, a division of HarperCollins Publishers,
1350 Avenue of the Americas, New York, NY 10019.
www.harperchildrens.com

Library of Congress Cataloging-in-Publication Data
Williams, Susan, 1953–
Wind rider / by Susan Williams. — 1st ed.
p. cm.
"Laura Geringer Books."
Summary: Fern, a teenager living in 4000 B.C., defies the expectations of her people by displaying a unique and new ability to tame horses and questioning many of the traditional activities of women.
ISBN-10: 0-06-087236-5 (trade bdg.) — ISBN-13: 978-0-06-087236-6 (trade bdg.)
ISBN-10: 0-06-087237-3 (lib. bdg.) — ISBN-13: 978-0-06-087237-3 (lib. bdg.)
[1. Human-animal communication—Fiction. 2. Horses—Fiction. 3. Sex role—Fiction. 4. Prehistoric peoples—Fiction.] I. Title.
PZ7.W66818Win 2006 2005028595
[Fic]—dc22 CIP
AC

Typography by Larissa Lawrynenko
1 2 3 4 5 6 7 8 9 10
❖
First Edition

For Cathy, who used to ride a pony
named Maple Sugar with me.

For Fern, who, one summer long ago,
wanted to be a cave girl.

For Spring, of the wise and beautiful eyes.

For all the horses and dogs
I have ever loved.

CONTENTS

WIND RIDER

CHAPTER ONE

BOG

"Where are you going, Fern?" Grandmother croaked in her dried-up-spider voice. "You fed that bird twice this afternoon already."

I sighed and rolled my eyes. Sometimes I could sneak away without Grandmother knowing, but other times she seemed to feel with her spirit the empty place where I had been. Old and blind she might be, but she was still one of the best workers in our *ahne*. Even as she asked the question, she cleaned and hung yet another fish, ignoring the stink and the smoke that made my throat close up and my eyes water. She moved like a branch that dips, bends, and dips again in the endless current of the river.

"Xj'i sah," I answered crossly. I did not really need to return my body's water to Earth Mother, but I had to get away. I paused a moment at our shelter to stroke the neck feathers of my baby crow, who was perched in the shady nest I had made for him between the cross poles. I had found him a few days before, under a tree, with his mouth wide open, showing me his red, hungry insides. My mother wanted to put him in the stewpot, but instead I fed him scraps of fish and named him Black.

It felt bad to lie to Grandmother, but not as bad as being stuck cleaning fish while my brother played in the river. I was supposed to be splitting fish—thumbing their guts into a heap, and sticking them on racks to cure in the sun and the smoke from our fires. After the snow melts, the first warm rains bring suckers swarming up the rivers in slippery herds. It is not such a large run as that of the salmon in the fall, or as tasty, but it is food. The five families of our *ahne* would be busy for several days.

Ahne means hand. I like to think about that. We move over the steppe, gathering what we can to feed our own life. When winter storms would swallow us, we go into the Earth herself, to the shelter of our pit houses. So *ahne* also means a group of families that travel together during the warm months, joined together like the fingers of a gathering hand.

It is strange how I remember everything about that afternoon. My mother, Moss, and her friend Rain sat talking together in the shade of our hut, each nursing a baby. Our Little Brother was teething. "Hush now, or the Night People will hear and steal you away," Rain scolded him. "They might be hiding in the bushes this very moment."

"Do not say such a thing!" my mother answered sharply. I saw her glance over her shoulder. The Night People live beyond the place where the sun sets. They are horrible. When Moss was a girl, a group of hunters from our *ahne* found her. She was hiding under the burned skins of her family's shelter—a bundle of bones with staring eyes. Everyone else was dead or stolen. For many days she could not even tell them her name.

Over in the river, some boys splashed beside the men who were catching fish in hemp nets. I could see my brother Young Flint looking into the water behind each rock, trying to spear a fish. It was too cold this early to wade very long, but boys want to spear something alive instead of an old skin target.

In many ways Flint and I are as different as the sun and the earth, yet like them as connected. He is not just my brother but my twin. We were the only twins in all the *ahnes*. Sometimes people whispered about us.

Choices, excitement, and honor lay ahead for Flint. I, on the other hand, would no sooner find blood running between my legs than I would be packed off to begin growing babies, tending pots, and scraping skins for some young man as reckless and stupid as my brother, who, like him, would not listen to anything I had to say. It was a black thought, yet when Flint yelled, raising his spear with a flopping fish on the end of it, I could not help grinning and calling out, "Good—it is a big one!"

I might have gone to the river's edge to laugh at my brother slipping and falling like a person who has drunk from a skin of fermented berry juice, but I was sick from fish stink, and I was sure I had hung enough suckers for ten summers' use. Besides, I told myself, they will forgive me when I bring home a basketful of fern sprouts.

Snatching an empty gathering basket from behind the tent, I started off. I heard my dog, Bark, get up and pad softly along behind me. Once away from the camp, Bark and I raced across the grassland to the clump of willows that marked the edge of the bog. We stopped in their cool shade, panting.

The bog lies where the river once curved like the

print of a horse's hoof. When my father, Old Flint, was a boy, a great storm led the river to find a shorter path, where it runs today. The ferns for which I am named can be found in the wet place that was left behind. Later in the season they would grow almost as high as my head, but now, all the way to the edges of the world, the steppe was barely touched with green. Earth Mother seemed to yawn and stretch, like a girl just waking up. Toads trilled and these same ferns were curled tight, like a baby's fist.

With the stench of fish behind me, my stomach growled at the thought of fern sprouts. I love them best boiled with a bit of fat melting over them. They are my favorite springtime food. When the land is frozen white and hard, and we wonder if it will ever be warm again, my mouth waters just thinking about them. In the season's first bellyful, I can almost feel the spirit of the plants uncurling inside me, green with life.

"Ferns are strong, but bending, beautiful, yet unmindful of their beauty," my mother always said to me when she caught me plaiting flowers into my hair and peering at my reflection in the water of the cooking pot.

"I would rather be named for something proud of its beauty that does not bow to the wind but flies with it—

like a horse," I would answer back, "not some stupid old plant."

Now I kept to the edges of the bog, remembering how once, when I was little, I got into the black muck over my knees and could feel it sucking like one of those fish we were drying, only so huge that I thought it would swallow all of me. I screamed until Moss found me and pulled me out with a branch. Then, instead of hugging, she cuffed me—but all the time tears streamed down her cheeks. I clung to her, furious at the spank yet desperate for the safety of my mother's arms.

Now I scrubbed my hands with mint leaves to get rid of the fish smell. Mosquitoes and midges swarmed around my head, crawled behind my ears and into my hair. "The Spirit of Life gave us biting insects so that when Sun Father transforms the land from harshness to beauty, we will know that we have not passed into the afterworld," Grandmother told me one time. I think we might have gotten the idea with half as many bugs.

Just ahead, I knew, I would find a large patch of sprouting ferns, but as I came around a willow tree, Bark growled and I saw broken reeds and torn earth, then the half-devoured body of a horse with the legs sticking stiffly up in the air.

I sniffed, smelling blood and torn-open guts, but not

the sickening stink of a rotting carcass. It was freshly killed, perhaps the night before. The horse had been chased into the soggy ground where it could not escape. I found huge cat tracks in the soft earth, but Bark stopped growling and tore hungrily at what was left of the hindquarters, so I knew the cat could no longer be near. I was just taking my knife out of its sheath to cut some meat to bring home to our cooking fire when something moved out in the bog. Something big and tawny—the cat? My heart pounded and I could not breathe. But no, it was another horse, a young one, just past its second winter.

When it saw me, it plunged and snorted. Its eyes rolled, showing white flashes of fear. Perhaps the mother was old, without a new baby, and so this one had still run beside her. Being smaller, it had stumbled farther out before becoming trapped, belly deep. Maybe the cat was satisfied with one kill. Maybe it was afraid of the bog. It had not tried to go after the smaller horse.

My brother Flint would have run all the way back to camp, bursting to tell about finding so much fresh meat. But the young horse quieted again and turned to look at me. Its eyes were big and afraid, its nostrils huge and blowing. I knew I could not do that.

Chapter Two

Dream

It looked as if a battle between two beasts had been fought there in the bog, but the battle had truly been between the young horse and the sucking earth. I snapped off some willow branches and laid them over the mud. Bark whined as I crawled out onto the branches. For once he did not follow. Twigs poked into my belly. One caught on the little bone amulet around my neck. Impatiently I tugged it loose and turned it on its thong so that it would hang down my back out of the way. My nose was filled with the oily, dead-plant stink that is the bog. The cold slime of it soaked through my clothing to my skin.

Suddenly I felt my knees and elbows sinking. Fear

clutched my belly. I had to crawl back to find more branches. All this time the horse eyed me watchfully. When I finally got within arm's reach, it squealed, plunging and thrashing like a storm in a forest. But it could go nowhere. Mud rained on me. I crouched, covering my head. Once I saw the underside of a hoof in front of my face and felt on my cheek the wind it made passing through the air.

After many heartbeats the storm died, and the horse lay still, sides heaving. I spoke to it then, softly. "I will not hurt you. I will help you." But how? I had no idea. If I asked anyone of our *ahne* for help, there would be a great horse roast that night. Then I reached out and touched the little horse's sweat-soaked rump. The skin quivered, but that was all. How long had it been trapped here? It must drink and eat or the bog would kill it as surely as the great cat had killed its mother.

There was a spring not far away. Peeling off my leather shirt, I lined the gathering basket with it and filled it with water. Getting the water to the horse, crawling over the mat of broken branches, was not easy. I lost some of it on the way. Then I clawed a pit in the mud near the horse's nose and set the basket of water there. But now the young horse stared beyond me with empty eyes. I pulled up fistfuls of grass, too, and left them beside the water. "Please do not be afraid," I whispered. "I want you to live."

Then I struggled back to solid ground, pulling the branches behind me so that no beast could get to it when I was not there. That was all I could think of to do. Bark had left his scent all around. He was big, larger than some of the wild dogs, and many animals were afraid of him. I hoped the little horse would be safe until I could come back. I piled the muddy branches over the body of the mare, hoping the cat would not return.

On the way home I washed the bog slime off in the river. I was scratched all over, and the water stung. With no shirt, I shivered. I pulled my amulet to the front again and stared at it.

On our Naming Day, Moss carved a fern for me on a disk of deer antler. Flint was proud of the tiny, perfectly knapped point he was given. But I had seen the amulets that Wolf and Bear wore. I sobbed. I did not want to be named for a plant; I wanted to be named for an animal. I woke and slept with the horse's tail that my father had given me for a plaything. It was horses I loved best.

Then Grandmother took the short bone from inside a hoof and carved it into a tiny mare with a curving neck and a rounded body. With the finest awl she had, she drilled a hole through its middle and strung it on a strong piece of sinew. Then she fastened it around my neck instead of the other.

"It seems we should have named you Hekwos for your love of horses," she said then, ignoring my mother's frown. "Perhaps since you think so much of wind runners, the Spirit of the Wind will watch over you." Then she held the horse so that I could see the tiny fern she had carved on its back, saying, "That is so you will not forget who you really are."

Now as I touched my amulet, my hands shook. As long as I could remember, I had watched horses. It was almost as if I were thirsty for them, drinking in their swiftness and beauty. But the only ones I had seen up close had been killed for meat. Today I had touched a living wind runner. Could it be that Hekwos was seeking me? The thought made me shiver.

It was nearly dark. I hurried back to the camp. Cooking fires were already blazing. I paused in the shadows outside my family's fire circle hearing my father ask, "Where is Fern?"

Grandmother rested her grindstone, squatting back on her skinny haunches. Her toes were bent from all the time in her long life that she had spent kneeling to grind roots and barley. "She slipped away to her own doings when we were cleaning fish," she told him. "I have not heard her dog bark for many long thoughts. She is not in the camp."

My mother said, "She must be watching the herds again or trying to catch some animal for a pet. I do not like it."

Then Grandmother said, "The child sees with different eyes. Her friendship with animals may be a gift."

Moss snorted. "Sometimes I think she is touched with darkness. No other child would talk to a grass snake or steal a half-grown marmot from her brother's snare and try to mend its broken leg or keep a frog in her gathering pouch. She may as well make a pet of this soup I am cooking."

My brother Flint would surely have spotted me slithering half naked under the edge of the tent to hunt for my other shirt, if he had not been busy helping Old Flint make preparations for a hunt. Everyone was sick of fish. A few scattered aurochs had been spotted near the edge of the forest land. The men might be gone for several days. Flint begged to go along instead of packing our father's carrying pouch with dried fish and a few handfuls of the last of our grain, as he was supposed to be doing. "I am big enough to hunt, truly I am," he pleaded.

Moss turned from where she was roasting a large sucker with onions over the coals. She pushed a strand of hair out of her eyes. "Sometimes hunters return torn and bleeding. Sometimes they do not return at all. Next year is soon enough for you to make your first hunt."

"But you saw how many fish I speared, Father!"

"It would be difficult to miss when they swim so thickly. I also saw the two good spears you broke," said Old Flint, rolling a sleeping fur into a tight bundle. His voice was stern, but the twitching at the corner of his mouth showed he was not angry. "It is no small thing to guard the camp. Because you are old enough to help with that, we can take along another hunter."

Silently I came out of the tent and stood a moment listening to see if they would talk about me again. Grandmother's head turned my way. She smiled to herself. It was no good hiding from Grandmother, so I stepped into the firelight.

"Where have you been?" my mother demanded. Little Brother, whining with swollen gums, clung to her so that she could work with only one hand.

"Into the tent and out again," said my grandmother, before I could answer. "And the dog named Bark, who prefers having his belly rubbed to hunting with the pack of camp dogs, has rolled in fish guts once more."

My face burned. "I went to find fern sprouts for my father's supper."

"And where are they?" my mother asked, seeing my empty hands.

"Not up yet," I mumbled. I took Little Brother from her, hoping she would be pleased by my helpfulness.

My father looked at me sharply. If he knew that I spoke untruth, he said nothing, but again his mouth twitched.

"Fahnie!" Little Brother crowed. He dropped the bone he was gnawing to grab my hair, but he did not let go of Wolfie, the tattered wolf tail that he carried everywhere. I motioned to Bark to lie down outside the fire circle where we could not smell him as much.

"But Wolfie does not stink," I said to Little Brother, pretending to stroke his pet. "Wolfie is good. Bark is a bad stinky boy." Bark made a sad sound in his throat, and Little Brother laughed.

He had not yet reached his Naming Day. Often little ones are taken back by Earth Mother, so we do not give them names until they have passed their third winter. Moss had lost more babies than most of the women in our *ahne*. I had seen another Little Brother and a Little Sister laid cold and still in the breast of the earth. Both times Flint and I had crawled into bed and crouched together, pulling our sleeping robes tightly over our heads, but we could not block out the endless wailing of our mother or the groans of our father, and we could not stop seeing memory pictures of each lifeless little body.

Grandmother had told me that two others, before Flint and I were born, died in Moss's belly. The lines around my mother's mouth were deep, and she did not laugh very much.

Now I took Little Brother to see Black. My baby crow made cross, muttering noises when I woke him, but he needed his supper and gulped it greedily. The firelight sparked in his eyes as he watched us between bites of smoked fish. He was a baby, but his eyes looked like a wise old man's. When he was full, he shook his feathers, shut his blue eyelids, which closed from the bottom up, and stuffed his head back under a wing.

Little Brother was sleepy now. I gave him back to my mother. Silently I ate my own food and began cleaning up the mess of the meal while my brother, copying Old Flint, lay back and relaxed. I scowled, remembering the untidy camp I had once seen of three men who lived without women. Half-eaten food lay about uncovered, with flies crawling on it. The ground around their fire pit was littered with bones and rubbish, tools and clothing.

A stink came from their bed furs as if they had never been washed or sweetened in the sun. The men smelled the same way.

Males were pigs, I thought. How could you make them share work that they did not even think needed to be done? Yet they would spend much time whittling a dart shaft or knapping the perfect point. Why did men get to do all the exciting and important things while women were left with the boring, dirty jobs? It must be wonderful to run freely over the steppe, leaving heavy shelters, cooking pots, and babies behind, to hunt and return to feasting and praise.

When he thought no one was looking, I saw my brother slip my dog a hunk of fish skin and ruffle the thick fur of his neck.

"Bark's tail moves that way because he likes you," I told him.

Flint jerked his hand away, thrust out his chin, and said, "Dogs are for tracking game, not petting. All other animals are meat."

Moss shook her head, saying, "I never saw a girl like you. Willow and Berry do not run off by themselves and carry home sick and injured animals to waste good food on. You talk to creatures as if they were people."

I swept ashes back into the fire pit so roughly that

some of them flew up into my face. "Maybe I like animals better than people," I muttered, blinking back tears.

Old Flint looked up and wrinkled his nose. "Your dog smells like a refuse pit, Fern. You must make him swim in the river tomorrow. I do not understand why he will not run on the hunt with the other dogs but must still play like a puppy and trail after a girl child as she learns women's tasks."

"Bark can catch game when he needs to!" I cried. I did not know what else to say. What my father said was true. But why should a dog be just a tool for hunting, like a spear or a knife? Could he not see that my dog had feelings too, that he loved to be petted and hugged and told he was a friend?

Even when he smelled good, Bark was not allowed to sleep in the tent with me. Moss had a stupid fear that he might eat Little Brother while we slept. That night, as I curled up in my sleeping robe, I was glad of it, for my dog did stink. Still, I liked the warm feel of his back pressed against mine through the side of the tent.

I could not sleep. Maybe right now some creature was attacking the young horse. Maybe the horse was too weak to live another night. If it did live, if I somehow got it out of the bog, what would I do? How could I hide a horse? And I must hide it, for if it were found, it would be dinner for sure. How could I keep the *ahne* from killing it?

Bark whined, sensing my restlessness. I reached under the edge of the tent and rubbed his ears. I thought about my dog.

When my friends Willow and Berry were playing babies with dolls made of felt and leather, I had taken a wriggling bundle of fur that was a puppy and had made it into my baby. I had stolen him from a big, friendly, yellow bitch who hung around our campfire. She would creep toward me on her belly when I threw her scraps. She did not growl or back away like most of the other dogs, but would sometimes let me rub her head. She had dug a den under a rock near our spring camp and had her puppies there.

I watched every day until she began to wean them. Then one morning when she was out hunting, I crawled into the den. In the shadows I could make out four puppies cowering against the rock wall. One came wriggling toward me making the foolish little yaps that would later become his deep, sharp call. *Bark.*

My friends squealed and my mother shook her head as I nuzzled the pup's soft fur, smelled his sweet puppy breath, and laughed when his tongue washed my cheek and he tried to suckle my ear. When I played Naming Day with him, Moss had looked sideways at Grandmother and said low, so she thought I could not hear, "It is not right to give a name to an animal. What if Sun Father is angered?"

But Grandmother had laughed and gazed into the air. Her eyes were like the water of the river when the children had stirred it up swimming, but I knew she still saw pictures inside herself. "Sometimes a new path leads to something good," she had said. "We can learn much from beasts. The Spirit of Life fills them, just as it fills us. Let the child play."

Then Grandmother had said to me, "Bring the dog, Bark, here so I can give him a Naming Day gift."

Bark came happily to my whistle. I pushed his bottom down to make him sit respectfully in front of my grandmother the same way I was taught to do when I was little. Then Grandmother held out a piece of dried deer meat and spoke to him just as if he were a little boy and not a dog. "Long life of joy and growing to you who are named Bark." That is what is always said when a name is given.

Then I could not believe my eyes. Bark, who ate all his food in great gulps, politely accepted the meat from her and waved his tail! I took Grandmother's hand and let her feel it moving so that she could see him thanking her.

At that time those words seemed crazy to me. Bark would soon be a big dog. He could not keep growing *all* his life, or he would be monstrous like the huge creatures with long tusks that roamed the steppe in the time before memory. Storytellers whispered about them to make our eyes grow wide. Grandmother had lived many winters. She grew more shrunken and dried up every year. Neither a person nor a dog could keep growing always!

As Bark got older, I learned that he would keep me safe. He told me when danger was near. With him I could walk far without being afraid. He talked to me with his eyes, ears, and tail. He made small noises in his throat that were not barks or growls. He groaned with pleasure when I rubbed his belly, whimpered to say that he wanted to go with me, sighed when he was bored.

If we were alone together, Berry sometimes petted my dog, but Willow didn't like him. She was always afraid he would bite her. She drew back and squealed when he tried to make friends with her. Willow was older. If she was there, Berry let herself be tugged away from me, while Willow whispered in her ear about "the dog-girl."

My mother shook her head and gave me black looks. But I could not help what I felt. Bark was my spirit friend. Wherever I went, he went. And whatever Moss said, I think that in her heart she was a little bit glad that Bark went with me.

That night I lay awake for a long time, staring into the darkness. How could one girl, not even a woman yet, save a horse from the bog? I heard a log in the fire outside break in two, and through the smoke hole watched the red sparks it sent up into the night. My father had left our door flap open a little for air. For a moment the fire flared, making running shadows on the wall of the tent. How I longed for the trapped horse to be free to gallop with the wind once more. I ached to fly with it, to escape this trap of being a girl. If only I could become a horse myself. . . .

Horses were running down from the high steppe into the river valley. The herd poured through one of the gullies that cut down to the flood plain. Their bodies gleamed like salmon backs in the sun. Dust rose in a brown smoke, and there was a rumble of their hooves striking the ground.

There were tens and tens and tens of horses, led

by a white-eyed mare and chased by a bellowing stallion. They came straight to the river, dropped down the bank, splashed to the other side, and disappeared into the grassland beyond. But one horse remained in the river. And now the water was not water but black mud, and the horse plunged and screamed but could not free itself.

Then I ran to the river, and it was strange, but I could walk over the mud and not sink down. When I reached the horse, it quieted. Then I looked, and my eyes saw the rounded hollow of its back and the long hair of its mane. I saw . . . and taking hold of the mane, I slid a leg over the horse's back. Then, together, we came out of the mud and the horse began to gallop. It did not hear the calls of the wild herd on the far side of the river anymore. It ran on my side of the river, alone, except that I was upon its back. Together we flew over the ground. . . .

When I woke up from the dream, it was just getting light. I bit my lip, thinking that this foolish dream had done nothing to tell me how to get the horse out of the bog. Maybe the cat had come back and killed it in the night anyway. Then everyone could stuff their bellies and the men would not need to go on a hunt. I battled inside myself. I should tell my father about the horse, for we never know, summer or winter, when hunger might be crouching near. But I could not make my heart listen to my conscience.

I rolled over and tugged up the side of the tent to look out. In the white mist of early morning, I watched as my father tossed a rope over the branch of a willow. I had seen him do this many times before. He tied a bundle of smoked fish, wrapped in rawhide, to the end of the rope. Next he pulled on the rope, using the strength of the tree to help him lift the bundle into the air where the beasts of the night could not get it. Without the tree and the rope, Old Flint could not have lifted the bundle so easily. Then, whistling the signal he used for his hunting dogs, he walked off into the mist to join the other men. The four dogs, with their tails curled over their backs, trotted at his heels.

Suddenly I grinned. I knew a way to help my horse—and in that instant I felt a rush of joy, for I knew for the first time that it was *my* horse.

My fine hunter of a brother still lay asleep, snoring softly. He had not even woken when Old Flint left. The others slept as well. Silently I dressed, planning what I needed and what excuse I would use when they questioned me later. But my mind was still full of the dream.

Chapter Three

FREE

The moment the hunters were out of sight, I was up and running to the bog. When Bark and I crept back to the willow tree and I looked past it to where the horse was trapped, my heart stopped for a moment because its eyes were closed and it lay so still. Then I saw its ribs move. It was sleeping. The water container was empty.

I laid the branches back over the mud. The horse struggled again as I was getting the basket, but not so much as the day before. I brought more water and then hid, watching. The sun moved almost a hand's width in the sky before the little horse, very cautiously, stretched its nose to the water.

Then it drank, and in a moment the container was empty. I brought more. This time the young horse looked eagerly for the water. And this time I put my hand out and touched its neck. It blew air through its nostrils but did not struggle.

I brought fresh grass, and it ate, just a blade or two at first, then more and more. The sun was overhead now. Moss would wonder where I was. Part of me wanted to stay with my horse, to try to pull it out of the bog right then. The other part knew that it was too soon. If it fought me, it might get trapped so deeply that I could never get it out, or if I managed to pull it out, it might run away. I had to gain its trust.

I filled the water container one more time, then hurried to fill the other basket I had brought with fern sprouts. I knew better than to leave a pile of grass that might shrivel in the sun for the horse. I remembered the bellyache I had once had from eating wilted greens. Thirst kills faster than hunger. My horse would be all right.

For the rest of the afternoon I cleaned fish, then mended a shirt of my father's to make up for Moss's raised eyebrows and silence. But I could not stop thinking about my horse.

If I did get it out, where could I hide it? A horse was

a very big animal. Then suddenly it came to me. There are many gullies running from the steppe down to the river. I knew of one so narrow and choked with brush that nobody but a girl trying to catch a crippled bustard chick that she had chased from the grassland would go there. A small stream of water trickled through it.

Not far from there was an abandoned camp. I had seen weathered tent poles scattered around the blackened fire pits. The opening at the bottom of the gully was so narrow that I might be able to block it off with those poles. I could make it into an enclosure for my horse!

Moss clucked her tongue, and I bent my head again over my work. I was not a good sewer, and I was especially clumsy with the awl. Sometimes I poked it too far and tore the hole to the edge. This time I snapped a good awl by twisting it impatiently, instead of rocking it back and forth. Then, when I was trying to force another point through a place where the leather was thick and tough, my tool slipped and I jabbed my thigh. "Uhhh!" I cried. The hole ached, but it barely bled.

Grandmother felt the wound and pressed the sides of it to make the blood flow. "If it does not bleed, such a wound will fester," she told me as she wiped it clean again. She was called Touch-Sees because her fingers were her eyes. They whispered over the surface of things, telling her almost as much as her eyes once had. I loved to feel the pads of her fingers tracing the curve of my lips when I was happy or touching a tear when I was sad. I tried to close my eyes to see things with my own fingertips as she did—a flower, a fish, my sewing—but my fingers could not see as Grandmother's did.

I threaded a bone needle with a length of sinew and continued the seam. Moss's eyes followed my work. My mother's sewing was beautiful. Not only were her seams straight and the stitches perfect, but she decorated everything. Even my father's mittens for winter hunting had a design of reindeer stitched to the back of them in red felt. She still had the tunic she had made for herself when she became his wife. She was only two winters older than I was now. Often young women came to her and asked to see it when they were beginning their own bridal tunics. They gasped and touched each bird and flower as if it had sprung alive from Moss's patient fingers. I used to be very proud of my mother's sewing, but now that I had to learn the task myself, I hated her skill.

After a moment Moss snorted, took the shirt away from me, and pulled against the seam, showing me all the gaps in my stitches. "The wind does not blow more gently because a girl sews carelessly," she said. "A hunter's life may depend on the seam that you sew." She began to yank my stitches out. I scowled but said nothing. My cheeks burned. I hated my mother! Soon I would have to learn to sew water pouches that would not leak and run dry. I wanted to cry. It was hopeless.

Grandmother must have known my thoughts, for when Moss went out, she said to me quietly, "Your mother is stern, but she loves you. Did you know that she fought to keep you when you were born. Do you see any other twins in the *ahne*? It is too hard to raise both, and it is not the girl child who is kept. But Moss had lost too many babies before. She would not listen. It is a wonder she had enough milk."

I stared at Grandmother. *Not the girl child who is kept?* I knew about Moss's stillborn babies, but not this. What was done with a baby that was not kept? Was it killed? Would I have been left out on the steppe for a hungry beast to find? But I did not have time to think any more just then, for my brother Flint came into the tent to fetch Old Flint's tools for knapping dart points.

"Tell your father that we need a new awl," Grandmother said to him.

Flint looked at me and grinned. He knew who had most likely broken a sewing tool. Then he spied the basket of fern sprouts. "If I took half a day to gather a basket of fern sprouts, Old Flint would pitch me into the river. Yesterday you said they were not up."

I ignored his last words. "If I took half a day to gather a few sticks of firewood, Moss would pitch *me* into the river," I spat back. I wanted to shove him into the river myself, but lately he had grown taller and stronger than me. I knew I would get a twisted arm or a mouthful of dirt if I tried. Bison turd of a brother! We might no longer be matched in strength, but I was determined he would never beat me with words.

Time dragged. Late in the afternoon Little Brother fell asleep. Flint disappeared, hunting rats along the riverbank with some other boys. The fish cleaning was done; only the fires needed to be tended to finish the smoking process.

"I think there is a grass hen nesting by the flat rock," I lied.

Grandmother shook her head and sighed. "Go, Fern. Soon enough you will be tied to babes and fireside."

I was already running. "Not me, ever!" I yelled back at her.

The sun burned hot, flies buzzed, and the stench of dung hung in the air when I reached the bog. The horse could not stay there much longer. It drank as soon as I brought water. It drank many times. I brought as much water as it would drink. Then I brought handfuls of grass.

A horse can eat a lot of grass. I could not stay long with darkness coming, but I brought grass until its hunger seemed duller. By now it had lost some of its fear of me. I stroked its neck while it ate. Most of the horse's rough winter fur had been shed, and the summer fur was sleek. I left the container filled with water and pulled all the branches away once more. How I wished that I could make a fire here and keep guard through the night! I could not bear to lose my horse now. I knew what I would try to do, but I needed daylight.

When I got back to the camp, the hunters still had not returned. Grandmother Touch-Sees was grinding roasted barley to make some of her small, hard loaves for our supper. I helped Little Brother string bone beads on a thong so that Moss could cook. The beads made a nice clicking sound. As Flint brought an armload of wood, Moss said, "I am missing a gathering basket and a good rope. Do you know anything about them?"

"Fern has a secret," he answered. "You might ask her."

"I do not," I said. "I have only been hunting turtle eggs near the bog." As soon as I said it, I knew my stupidity. Turtles would not lay their eggs for at least another moon change, and the bog was the last place I wanted my brother snooping.

Flint smirked and snatched a fistful of grain from the hollow of Grandmother's grinding stone, but Grandmother caught his wrist in midair with a hand like a bird's claw, saying, "Steal no more of my grindings, young weasel!"

He scuttled out of her reach, stuffing his mouth. My brother was a lot like my crow, Black. "My knows-all-things sister says feather grass sprouts in the winter, too," he chortled with his mouth full. I threw a handful of cold ashes at him. Little Brother squealed and bounced in my arms.

Moss frowned. "You know well that those things are the work of many days. I want them found."

I pretended to be very interested in stringing Little Brother's beads. I could probably get the basket back soon even if I could never get all the mud washed out of it, but I needed the rope.

After our supper, Moss took Little Brother and nursed him to sleep crooning the song about the Moon Child who grows and shrinks and is born over and over again, from the love of Earth Mother and Sun Father:

Sleep now, little one,
Your face as round and bright
As the moon. . . .

It was the very same song she used to sing to Flint and me when we were small, as we crowded together in her lap, each nestled in one of her strong arms.

I watched Grandmother dozing, crumpled into herself like a dried root. The firelight deepened the creases of her face. It seemed sad to me that the shorter the time Grandmother had left to live, the more of it she spent asleep. But as I watched, she smiled at something in her dreaming. Was her dream life a bright time away from the stiff joints and endless darkness of her waking life?

Flint, looking very important, took a brand from the fire and walked around to the other tents to talk to Old Sun Dog and Hawk, the two men who had been left in charge of the *ahne*. Hawk was a hunter, but despite his fierce name, he often chose to stay behind because he liked the chance to work on his beautiful bone carvings and, like his father before him, to think up stories to tell us children.

It was easy to slip into the tent and help myself to several handfuls of barley kernels. If Flint could steal grain, so could I. The bag was slack. It would be several months before the barley heads would hang heavy once more for gathering. I felt a twinge of guilt, but saving my horse was important.

The next morning I crept away once again, but I did not go straight to the bog. First I went to the old camp and dragged all the poles I could find to the mouth of the gully. Then, with a hand axe, I hacked a space in the brush so that the horse could move around a little and get to the water.

Afterward, as I approached, the horse made a sound in its throat, *Hhhhhhhhhnnnnn.* I had heard mares make that same welcoming sound to their foals when they came to their sides for milk. My heart sang.

I could see the tracks of three small wild dogs in the mud at the edge of the bog. I breathed a sigh of relief. That was as close as they had dared to go. I had made a loop of one end of my mother's braided leather rope. Tucking it under my shirt, I crawled out on my mat of branches.

The handful of grain was in the carrying pouch at my waist. As quietly as I could, I emptied some barley kernels into my hand and crushed them to make their smell stronger. Then I held my hand out. The horse would not have tasted grain since last fall, and never a winnowed handful.

The horse stared at me. I did not move. Much time passed. Bark crouched under a bush, watching. Once he whined. Finally the horse's muzzle reached toward my hand. It smelled the barley. I felt a tickling, as its lips found the grain. Then it shifted its weight away from me and chewed. I could see the tips of its jawbones working in the hollows above its eyes.

There are always bones and skulls near the places where the *ahnes* camp. I had seen how long and heavy the jawbones of horses were, how the teeth fit into their sockets, how they were worn short in the skull of an old horse. Although I had watched horses many times, I had never been so close. This was only a young horse, but it was so big, so powerful! My heart beat like a drum in my ears. I could feel the horse's breath warm on my hand. It smelled sweet, like steppe grass. I almost thought I could hear its heart beat too, a slower, deeper thump than my own.

Was it really me doing this thing? For a moment it was as if I were outside of my own body watching myself crouching beside this great beast. The horse nodded its head as it finished chewing and reached for another mouthful. As it was licking the last pieces from between my fingers, I slipped the rope over its ears.

It jerked up its head, muscles twitching at the rope as if it were a fly. After a time, when nothing happened, it began to look for the water and grass that I always brought. I fetched these things. Now I stayed beside it, smoothing my hand along its neck and talking softly while it drank and ate. Its ears moved back and forth, listening. Perhaps it was time.

Quietly I crawled back and looped the end of the rope around a thick willow branch. Then I began to pull steadily, turning the horse's head toward me. Bark paced back and forth, looking from one to the other of us and whining. At first the horse snorted and tried to struggle when it felt the tug of the leather, but then it saw the firm ground. The rope seemed to give the horse a way to try. It heaved and plunged toward me. I clenched my jaw together and used all the weight of my body. Then suddenly the horse's wind was cut off and it panicked, throwing itself sideways.

I slithered forward, scratching and jabbing myself on broken sticks. I do not know how I managed to loosen the rope, but the horse's gasp as it sucked air again was the best sound I had ever heard. Still I did not take the rope away. Somehow I felt that it was like a thought joining me to my horse. My strength was weaker, but my thought could make the horse stronger.

I felt sick inside to have frightened my horse so much. It must have believed that after all I was a hunter set on killing it. For a long time I sat beside it, spoke to it, sang Little Brother's sleep song, and stroked its neck. Finally the wildness left its eyes.

It took me a while to figure out how to fasten the rope to the horse's head so that it would not be choked again. It was a little like trying to find the best way to bind up a sleeping fur. Finally I made a small loop with a knot that would not slip, and slid it over the horse's muzzle. Then I passed the rest of the rope over its ears and down through the loop on the other side.

The horse trembled but was quiet. I talked softly. "You want to come out, do you not? You are my horse now, just like Bark is my dog. Will you follow me like he does?"

I thought of my dream then, and for a long moment I crouched beside the horse staring, without moving. Then, almost as if I were still in the dream, I leaned over the horse's withers. It listened to me with its whole body, the way Grandmother listens to a far-off sound. It did not fight. Slowly I slid my leg over its back until I was sitting upright, my shins resting in the mud. The horse felt my weight and quivered. Again I stroked its neck.

"You are a good horse. You are my friend. I will call you Thunder, for the sound that your feet make, galloping in my dreams. You will gallop once more. I will help you." Its ears turned toward my voice.

I slid back to the mat of branches, back to the hard ground, looped the end of the rope around the tree, and pulled again. The horse's neck went out straight, but this time it could breathe. It did not panic. It plunged and came forward an arm's length. Then, rearing, it freed a foreleg from the muck, bringing it down onto the branches. It was helping me!

Slowly, one leg at a time, the horse found something to push against. I did not have the strength to pull a horse, but I did have the strength to help a horse pull itself! It plunged and reared, but not in terror. It was working now, working toward freedom. It stopped and rested, panting. Its belly was nearly clear.

Then once again I leaned against the rope and the horse plunged. There was a sucking sound as the great, black fish of the bog finally released its prey. The horse staggered to the hard ground.

Bark bounded and yipped until I told him to hush. For long moments the young horse and I stood exhausted, panting, staring at each other. I could see now that she was female, ribs showing with hunger, black with bog slime. I too was covered with mud. Softly, I began again to sing the Moon Song:

Hush, my little one,
Fear no storm or beast,
I will keep you safe.
Shine, my little one,
With your own sweet light.

Then slowly, still trembling, I walked up to my horse and put my arms around her neck.

CHAPTER FOUR

LEARNING

When her ribs stopped heaving, the horse I had named Thunder bumped me with her nose, as if I were in the way, and reached down to tear great hungry mouthfuls of muddy grass. I did not want her to see the body of her mother, so I pulled her away from it toward a patch of clean grass. At first she leaned against the rope, not understanding what I wanted. But she was no longer afraid of me. She did not fight. I tugged back. She lowered her head and followed. She grazed for a long time.

Finally, she lifted her head and made a horse call, *Whehehehehehehehehe.* When there was no answer, she bumped at me again. Was she asking me to be her new mother, or maybe her leader?

"This way." I headed for our hiding place. Sometime I would show her to the *ahne*, I thought, but not yet. They would see her only as meat. I could have let her go, and chased her until she galloped off to the herd, but she was *my* horse now.

At first she would not follow me. Desperately I yanked hard on the rope around her head. It worked! Again the rope told her where to go. Steadily, stopping only to fill her mouth with grass from time to time, Thunder followed me. "Hurry," I begged her. "If anyone finds you, you will be killed!"

She stopped at the mouth of the gully until she saw the clearing I had made in the brush. I showed her the trickle of water, took the rope from her head, and while she was drinking, fixed poles and branches across the opening so she could not escape. I did not know how long I could keep her there, or whether she could protect herself from beasts.

The mud on her body was drying now. Before I left, I scraped away as much of it as I could. She shivered at the touch of my hands but was too tired to resist. As I worked at the crumbling mud on her left hindquarter, a patch of white hair emerged, as big as my two hands spread out, and shaped like the wings of an eagle. I sucked in my breath sharply, feeling a prickling at the back of my neck. The rest of her looked no different from any other horse, dun colored with charcoal stripes running down her spine and across her shoulders, a short, bushy mane of black hair, and black tail. My heart thumped as I smoothed the glistening white hairs with trembling fingers. I had never seen a horse marked with white. What did it mean?

I do not know what would have happened next if my father had not taken my brother with him to gather good flint from a gravel bank several days' walk away. Perhaps I never would have learned what I did then about my horse. I could escape many eyes, but not those of my brother, once he thought I had a secret.

My mother was cross with me all the time. Little Brother was very fussy. Moss tried again and again to give him to me or Grandmother to tend, but nothing seemed to comfort him except sucking restlessly, while his feet kicked and his free hand thumped fretfully against her breast. Grandmother could sometimes soothe him by giving him a knot of rawhide or a sweet root to chew, but he twisted and pushed away from me, screaming if I tried to hold him.

"If only you could gentle Little Brother the way you

do a puppy or a bird," Moss said with a sigh as she took him back. "I do not know what sort of mother you will make."

Her words stung like branches whipped in my face. I said the worst thing I could think of.

"Maybe I will not choose to be a mother. I hate babies! Why should I clean dirty bottoms just because I am female?" As soon as I said it, I felt sorry, for nothing was as sweet as Little Brother when he was clean and contented. But I would not take it back. I was too angry.

Her eyes darkened. "We do not get to *choose* child-bearing. Do not tempt Earth Mother with such words!" she growled. "This is my punishment for keeping you when you were born. No man will want you if you are always avoiding work and running off to your secret doings. You speak more to animals than you do to people! Go then." She almost spat the words at me.

So it was true. My mother was sorry that she had not let me die. I swallowed hard. Could it be that there really was something wrong with me? I looked at Grandmother, but she sat silently, staring inward. Usually she did not take either my side or my mother's, yet she did not try to stop me from slipping away every chance I got. As I twisted around to get up and run out of the tent, I felt Grandmother's hand on my arm. Her touch told me that she understood. In that moment I was sure that she had once been angry and maybe had felt unwanted—just like me.

In a day or two Thunder had gobbled up every leaf and blade of green stuff in the gully. I brought her armfuls of long grass, but that was not enough. I shook with fear the first time she let me fasten the rope over her head to lead her out to graze. What if she reared and bolted away, as horses did when the hunters tried to corner them? I had seen horses kick and bite each other. Would she do that to me?

Both of us were nervous. I was afraid that I might be killed by this great animal, and I was also afraid that someone would see my horse and try to kill her. Thunder stamped a foot, whinnying and listening for others of her own kind. But after a while she grew quieter, eating steadily, only flicking an ear and swishing her tail now and then.

After what seemed like a very long time, I gave a gentle pull on the rope and whispered, "That is enough for now, Thunder." Thunder tugged impatiently away from me and kept on eating. "Please," I said. "It is time to go back." I tugged again. The horse pulled back harder. Tears started in my eyes. Now Bark got up from the grass, the fur between his shoulder blades bristling. Thunder eyed him and snorted. Bark growled softly.

I took a breath, closed my eyes, and yanked as hard as I could on Thunder's rope, expecting slashing teeth, a horse scream of rage, and the sound of her hooves thundering away from me. In that same moment Bark made a dash at her legs! Thunder's head came up, and she jumped forward with a grunt, making the rope grow slack. I had taken one or two running steps when I turned and realized that the horse was following me. She was not angry! She was not fighting me!

Could it be that she just needed to be pushed like a stubborn child? Could it be that Thunder believed the rope and I were stronger than she was? I smiled to myself. Had we not pulled her from the bog? She did not know that she had mostly done it herself. I called Bark to me and patted his head. It was good to have a friend help me with my horse.

After that I brought Thunder out to graze as often as I could. She tore hungrily at the grass while I rubbed her coat with a twist of dried stalks. In a few days she grew round again, and her body shone like polished wood. The mark on her hindquarter was as white as the winter steppe. I liked to trace the shape of it with my finger. Sometimes I would lean against her warm side, praying no one would find us, my head filled with my strange dream.

In my mind we flew together, away from the bog, my angry mother, and my stupid brother, knowing only speed, freedom, joy. I wanted to see her run again, to know how fast she could move. I wanted to see her muscles working, to hear her feet pounding and her lungs drinking the wind. I wanted to run with her. I wanted to be part of her.

I ran my hands over her body, which was hard and strong, yet warm and smooth. I untangled her tail with my fingers and scratched the places on her belly and under her jaw where flies chewed at her. She let me rub the bug bites on the insides of her ears, and slide my fingers into her mouth and open it to look at her tearing teeth in front and her grinding teeth in back. Between the front and back teeth were gaps with no teeth at all. I wondered why that was.

Then I caught my breath. Was this a new way to join a rope to my horse without strangling her? I slipped a noose onto her lower jaw, over the front teeth and under her tongue, and let it rest across the gap. She chewed a little at the new thing in her mouth, stretching her lips wide like a yawning dog, until I laughed. Then, finding she could still eat, she ignored it.

Could I actually lead Thunder by her jaw? I pulled her head up and turned her one way and then the other. The rope told her what to do. I led her forward and then pulled at the rope to make her stop.

I remembered my dream. A voice, like wind in the spring grass, whispered, *See the hollow of her back, her long neck hair, the gap in her teeth—the horse was made for this! Why has no one seen it before?*

I was trembling. Hardly knowing what I was doing, I led Thunder to a fallen log. She rubbed her head against me, telling me that she was my friend.

"I am your friend too," I whispered. Then I climbed upon the log and slid onto the back of my horse.

Her head went up, and her ears twitched. Her whole body listened to me.

I sat there long enough to feel the strength of Thunder beneath me and to see the world as if I were very tall. This was different from the time I'd crawled onto her back when she was trapped in the bog. Then she had been helpless. She was free now, except for me and the rope, and she knew it. Her muscles quivered. Would she run?

She did not.

Her back was broad and warm, and my legs fit into the hollows between her shoulders and belly as if they were meant to be there. But I was not without fear. I had seen horses buck and rear. I might be thrown to the ground at any moment. Then it seemed as if it was time to get off, and I slid to the earth, both laughing and crying. My legs shook as if I were very cold.

Maybe I *was* some strange animal-talker person! Who in all the wide world had ever sat upon a living horse? I covered my mouth with both my hands and tried to breathe slowly again. Was it wrong? Was I touched with darkness, as my mother had said?

No, I told myself. *Thunder is good and beautiful. The Spirit of the Wind has shown me this thing. Hekwos watches over me. It is not wrong!*

The next day I climbed on Thunder's back again. After a moment she put her head down to graze. I knew then that she was not angry with me for sitting upon her. I smiled. She ate for a while. Then I pulled on the rope and made her head come up. She spoke back to me with little tugs of her jaw, telling me that she still wished to eat. But I remembered something. When the lead mare tells the herd to stop grazing and follow, they sometimes snatch another mouthful or two, but in the end they always mind her.

Thunder had asked me to be her lead mare. She believed I could be her leader, so I decided that even from her back, I must try. I held my breath and spoke to her with a stronger tug, again remembering all the fearful things a horse might do. To my amazement, she just raised her head from the grass and walked forward a few paces before putting her head down to eat again.

I wanted her to walk farther. I pulled her head back up. How could I tell her to walk? I did not speak horse language. But Bark understood a few words like *come*, and *down*, and *stay*, even if he could not make the sounds of the words himself. Could a horse learn the meaning of some of my words too?

"Walk," I said. She paid no attention to me. How could I make her go forward while sitting on her back and teach her the word at the same time? If only I had a person to help me. Then my legs did something without my thought telling them to. They pushed against her sides at the same time that I said the word. *Sun Father, she would throw me to the ground now!* But she did not. She moved forward. My legs talked to her! With the rope, and my voice, and now my legs, I told her not to eat again. I told her to walk toward the river, then away from it, to stop. She did all those things for me.

I laughed, turning my face to Sun Father, feeling wonder and joy. A horse, a creature of strength and speed, but also a prey animal who lived by fear, had not only learned to trust me but was willing to let me, a small human, tell her what to do.

Thunder learned more. The eagle rides the wind and cries a call that falls to the earth like sharp stones. My whistle for Bark was one long high note and four short lower notes. I learned it from one of the little birds that hide among the willow thickets in summer. But the horse and the eagle were both born from the Spirit of the Wind. So the eagle's cry, tumbling out of the sky, became Thunder's whistle, and it was not long before she would come to it.

I taught her to stop and then to walk forward again, from the ground as I walked beside her, and also from her back. One day when Thunder was carrying me, she heard distant whinnying from a herd of horses on the far side of the river, and broke into a trot before I could stop her. The bones of her shoulders and haunches pitched me around like tumbling water. I felt myself slipping sideways. Desperately, I grabbed Thunder's mane and pulled myself back upright. If I went off her now, she would surely run back to the herd! I tugged at her mouth until finally she came to a stop.

When the trembling left my body, I remembered my dream. But I did not dare to let her run again with the herd so near. I did not breathe easily until she was back in her enclosure in the gully.

The next time I climbed on her back, when I was sure no other horses were close, I felt braver. Cautiously I took hold of Thunder's mane and the rope and squeezed her with my legs. She trotted a few steps and stopped. I dug the heels of my feet into her sides, and this time she kept trotting while I struggled to keep my balance. Suddenly a hare bounded in front of us. Thunder shied, and I was dumped onto the ground. I scrambled up, running, expecting my horse to be gone, but the greedy thing stood there eating as if nothing had happened. Then I was shaking. So it had happened. I had fallen off. My knee was bruised, but that was all.

I grabbed her mane and swung myself back up. "We will try that again," I said to her.

Once again I asked Thunder to trot; but as soon as she started bouncing under me, I began to slide off again, and it took just a small shrug of her shoulders to send me face-first into the dirt. I spat blood where I had bitten my tongue, crying, not because it hurt so much as because I thought Thunder did not want me on her back.

Many days we practiced that way, but every time I asked Thunder to run with me on her back, I landed on the ground. What was I doing? I pounded my fists and sobbed into my arms. But then I would get up, catch my horse, and try it again. Still Hekwos must have watched over us, for I did not break any bones and Thunder did not run away.

Grandmother found my skinned elbow and a lump on my forehead one day when I flinched at her touch. "Is there something you should tell me about?" she asked me quietly.

I shook my head. "It is something good, something wonderful, but I cannot tell you now."

"I hope this good and wonderful thing does not break your neck," she said, shaking her head.

My father and brother returned with much good flint, but now they were busy working it into points and knives to put away for the autumn hunts. Moss thought I was a lazy girl who avoided work, perhaps even a witch who spoke in barks, howls, and grunts to animals. Let her think what she wanted! So long as I could get away to my horse, I did not care. And Grandmother, bless her old bones, seemed to trust me without asking any questions. She took Little Brother when I should have, finished my unfinished chores, and even covered my absences by claiming she had asked me to hunt the bone-healing plant or fever bark when she had done nothing of the sort.

Still, I was careful to keep my horse hidden and get on her back only when I was sure no one would see us, sometimes in the early morning, sometimes after each family was gathered by its own fire in the evening. I do not know what made me so stubborn. It was good to sit on Thunder's back while she walked steadily over the ground, but I could not forget my dream. I would not give up. I thought of how the boys practiced throwing spears until they could hit a target time after time and how Moss made me stitch the seams of Old Flint's shirt over and over again until it would keep out the hungriest winter wind. "More stitches, and closer, do it again," she always said.

It was strange to be learning something that nobody in all the *ahnes* had ever learned before. When I was little, I believed that *my* world, the huge circle that I could see around me, was all there was. Then one day a trader came to us. I pressed under the grown-ups' elbows, into the center of the crowd, and listened and stared. I could not understand much of his speech, but he used hand signs. I saw pictures in my head of strange places, cold northern forests, lakes so bitter with salt that nothing can live in them, and heights of land that touch the sky and are called mountains. He opened his pack and I saw shells, strange colored flints, lumps of glowing amber, rare herbs, and stones as blue as the night sky with tiny flecks in them like stars.

Sometimes when I was on Thunder's back, I would carefully raise myself until I was standing. Then I could see far over the tall grasses to where the earth and sky met in a hazy line. I could see *kolki*—patches of trees. I could see the river winding through the low grasslands, and the skin huts of the *ahne*. Hard as I looked, I could not see beyond my world to those strange lands. But I knew they were there.

Earth Mother is very large, very *omu*. Yet never, in all the nights of my life, as I sat listening by the fire, had I heard of a person riding upon the back of a horse.

One day Raven and his sons captured a horse in a pit trap and shared a shoulder joint with us. When Moss handed me my portion, my traitor nose drank in the delicious smell, and my mouth watered, but I clenched my jaw. Thunder was my friend—how could I eat one of her sisters? I slipped back from the firelight and began feeding the meat to my dog, who accepted it greedily.

Then my hand stopped. Bark was Thunder's friend too. But Bark needed to eat. And so did I. *Life for life.* The Spirit does not allow waste. I ate the meat, but I decided that when I was a woman, I would find a man who understood the feeling I had for my horse. We would not choose horse meat if we had other.

Day by day Thunder and I learned together, but I could not hide my horse forever. Often, when I was slipping away from the camp after hurrying to finish my share of work, I would catch my brother watching me. I had to walk far out of my way, seeming to be gathering basket reeds or greens, until Flint lost interest and stopped following me.

One afternoon Thunder carried me up the trail that the horse herd has followed since the morning of the world, and far out onto the steppe. Bark trotted beside us with his tail curled up over his back, his tongue hanging to the side and a dog grin on his face. Every way I turned my head, the many kinds of grasses bent and rippled in the endless wind. All the shades of green moved and swam together like water in the sunlight: greens the color of cat's eyes, duck's wings, thunderstorm skies, and pine groves. The fullness of it all made my throat ache with joy.

I could see where gusts of wind turned the blades of grass so that they showed their undersides in silvery, running waves. There were flowers too, scattered all the way to the edges of the earth. Over all this, cloud shadows raced like great blue fish.

My hair and Thunder's tail streamed in the wind. I breathed in the tangled smell of the grass-covered earth. My shoulders felt warm as Sun Father loved Earth Mother on this sweet day. Bark scented a hare and tore off until I saw only the grass tossing where he ran.

Would Thunder pitch me off again if I asked her to run? Fear gripped my belly and I began to breathe quickly. But the grass was long and soft here. What was one more tumble? Had I not hit the ground so many times I could hardly count them now?

I asked Thunder to trot. Her feet danced. I could feel her happiness. My legs were stronger. I balanced more easily, and she had learned to move more smoothly so that I did not bump on her back. We were doing it! She was trotting and I was staying with her! Then my dream came into my head, stronger than any fear.

"Run!" I called to her, and dug my heels into her sides. Thunder had not galloped since before she was trapped in the bog. Her shoulders surged up under me, her quarters tucked in from behind, and she *ran*!

I clutched her mane. Thunder ran in a horse's dance, like a woman rocking a child. It was easier than trotting! But suddenly her joy burst out like hot rocks exploding in a fire. Her head went down, and her feet flew up behind her. I was launched like a spear from its throwing stick. I landed on one shoulder and rolled over twice on the ground.

There was no breath in me. For a long moment I thought I was walking to the spirit world. Then finally I gasped air. Tears sprang out of my eyes. Above me the sky whirled in a blue-and-white circle. Carefully, I moved each arm and leg to see where I was broken. My shoulder ached, but that was all. Then a shadow fell over me. It was Thunder, nosing and asking why I was lying on the ground. In another moment Bark was on top of me, slapping my face all over with his tongue.

"Arrgh! Get off me, you wolf!" I pushed Bark away and struggled to my feet. I took hold of Thunder's rope bridle with both hands and scolded her: "You bad horse! You cannot play like a silly foal when I am on your back. Do you want me broken like an old cooking pot?"

Thunder just rubbed her face against me and stamped a hoof as if to say, "Hurry and get back on, it is a good day for galloping."

I did get back on. The second time Thunder did not buck. She stretched her head out and her feet flew, swishing, through the grass, scattering grasshoppers, flower heads, and small birds. At first Bark raced ahead of us. He glanced over his shoulder in surprise as Thunder overtook him. Then he lowered his head and ran as hard as he could to keep up. Now and then Thunder snatched at a grain head as she ran, and I threw back my head and laughed. "It is a very greedy horse who tries to gobble her supper as she gallops!" I called.

Thunder's muscles swelled and rolled under me, but I was safe on her back. I had found balance. She had found control. We moved with each other. A word came into my mind. I knew well the word *carry.* It was a thing my people did all the time. But being on Thunder's back when she ran was so much more than being carried! This thing of moving with the horse, as a bird soars with the wind, had never had a word. And now it did: *ride.*

I looked up into the blueness above and saw an eagle soaring on wide wings. It was racing us. A shiver ran down my spine. The messenger of Sun Father was watching us, flying with us. I closed my eyes, feeling the smooth motion of Thunder's body, hearing the rhythm of her breathing and the drumming of her hooves beating the earth. Who was the one with magic? Me or this horse who had learned to listen to me? We had learned each other's languages. We were part of each other, one spirit flying over the body of Earth Mother, under the warmth of Sun Father, with the blessing of Eagle above.

CHAPTER FIVE

USE

Later, just as I had returned Thunder to her hiding place in the gully, Bark spoke to tell me that someone was near. I heard my brother's voice: "There you are, dog-that-follows-females. Where is my sister?" He was still hidden by the grasses. My heart hammered in my chest as I drew the poles of the enclosure back into their places. Softly, softly, I ran toward the river, then turned back, so that when I approached my brother, he would believe that was the direction I had come from. I slowed to a walk and began humming Grandmother's basket-weaving tune. I could still hear him talking to Bark. His voice was kinder now. "Good dog, tell me where Fern is. What is this new secret that keeps her away so much?"

Oh the misery of brothers! How did he always know when I had something to hide? I tried to think quickly. What would fill his thoughts more than a secret of mine? Belly thoughts! No one, except Black the crow, was more greedy than my brother.

He heard my song. "There you are! I tracked you to the bog and the rain has washed away most of it, but I could see where there has been a big fight and there is the rotten, half-eaten carcass of a horse that would have fed the whole *ahne* for many days."

"Yes, well, it was rotten—what should I have done? But I know where there is a honey tree."

I could almost see his tongue working in his mouth.

"Where? Is it enough so that we need a carrying pouch? Should I run back for coals to make a smoke fire?"

"It is that way. We can use your shirt to carry it in. I have a fire kit in my pouch," I lied. What would I do when I got him that far? I did not know, but I had to get him away from the gully fast.

Flint strode ahead of me—he would never let me forget that he was the male—and I directed him to a small *kolki* a short distance away. "Old Flint will be pleased if I have found honey," he said eagerly.

"We," I corrected him, knowing full well that there was no honey to be had but not about to let him get away with such talk. *He will try to hit me, and I will have to run very fast when he learns of my trick,* I thought. Flint looked up at a twisted pine.

"I will climb up and see if I can spot the hunters coming back," he said. My brother was a good climber. Soon he was far up, like a squirrel. I could see the branches shake and the tree sway as he reached the top. I squinted against falling needles and bits of bark. There was a pause as he searched the distances all around for the hunters.

"Do you see them?" I shouted.

"No," he called back. He began to climb down. Suddenly there was a crack, and my brother hurtled through the branches and thumped on the ground. I think he saw blackness for a while, for he did not speak at first when I shook him.

"Are you hurt?"

"Eh, I am not," he said, starting to get up; then, "Argh—I am." He fell back, and I saw that the lower part of his right leg was bent where it should not bend. Blood ran from a wound on his forehead. Once again he tried to sit up, but again his head sagged. "My stomach swims—"

"Lie still," I told him. My stomach swam too. We were far from the *ahne*. I could not carry Flint, and if he could not walk, I would have to leave him. It would be dark before I could bring help. Anything could happen—a bear, wolves. An injured boy would make an easy meal. If only I had really brought a fire kit with me. A fire might have kept him safe until I could bring help. Even if I could somehow drag my brother home myself, the going would be so slow that there would be a long time of traveling in the dark. The skin at the back of my neck prickled. Could Bark fight off an attacking beast?

Then I remembered Thunder. "I will get you home."

"You cannot carry me—" Flint began, but I turned and trotted away. When he saw me leaving him, his voice rose almost to a scream. "Do not go! Your dog will not stay with me, and I will be eaten!" But I was off at a run.

Thunder tossed her head, happy to come out of her hiding place again so soon. I slipped the rope over her jaw. She wanted to eat, but when I leaped on her back, pulled her head up, and beat my heels into her sides telling her to gallop, she did. I did not take joy in it this time, for my belly was too full of dread that perhaps my brother's skull was broken as well as his leg. I thought that he might even this moment be walking alone to the spirit world.

As we came to the trees, I sat back and pulled on Thunder's jaw rope. "Walk," I told her. She was excited and danced a horse's dance of joy, but I was able to tug her head down. "You *must* walk," I told her, and now she obeyed. Flint was crouched against the pine tree, holding his spear, his eyes wild at the sound my horse had made moving through the brush.

When he saw the horse, with me on her back, he gave a yell of terror and threw his arms over his face. "She will not hurt you," I called to him, but he was crying and babbling like a crazy person.

"It is true. You are a witch!" he gasped between great shuddering breaths.

I leaped to the ground and turned to him. "I am only me," I said. "And she is only a horse, but I think a special one, given to me by Earth Mother and Sun Father. She will not hurt you."

He staggered upright on his good leg then, flexing his spear. I laughed, but inside myself I thought my brother brave to be ready to fight a big animal, alone and injured as he was. He smiled shakily. "Our father will be pleased. That is much meat. Get back so I can kill it!"

I flung myself in front of Thunder. "No!" I cried. "This is *my* horse. If you try to hurt her, I will leave you here for the wolves! Besides, you cannot brace yourself to make a good throw with a broken leg, stupid." Then I told him about the bog, the rope, and how I had brought water and grass to Thunder until she was not afraid of me, and then how I helped her out of the mud.

"But how did you keep her from running away?"

"I made an enclosure of poles for her in a small gully near the old camp. Look! She will carry you home. Her name is Thunder." Then I swung myself onto Thunder's back. Flint stared and wiped a hand over his eyes.

"It is as if you and the horse are . . . one animal. Am I seeing a dream picture?"

I made a sound with my mouth, squeezed my legs, and Thunder moved forward. I pressed against her side with one leg and pulled a little with the rope, and she turned in a circle, first one way, then the other. I stopped her and jumped off. Thunder rubbed her head against my arm. "And just now, she ran like the wind, with me on her back!" I said.

"But sooner or later something will eat her."

A shadow passed over my heart. "Yes, but today she will carry you home, and we will show the *ahne* that she has a better use than roasting. See! The Spirit of Life made her to carry us. There is a dip in her back here for us to sit, and long hair here, to hold on to, and look, even a gap in her teeth to pass a rope through to guide her. The rope talks to her; so do my legs and mouth. She listens to my thoughts, too. She does not wag her tail like a dog, but she rumbles a greeting when I bring her handfuls of grass or grain."

Flint's face was white as I helped him onto Thunder's back, and I do not think it was only from the pain in his head and leg. "You will not make her run?" he asked. He clutched her mane and gasped once when I began to lead her forward. Then he clenched his jaw and made no sound at all until we reached camp.

The hunters had returned. When they saw us coming, there were running feet and cries of fear. A girl screamed. I heard the sound of indrawn breaths and a moaning that was like an animal's sound of terror. I stopped Thunder. I did not know what to do. "It is all right," I called. "Do not be afraid."

The men of my *ahne* stood as still as if they had died upon their feet. Women, clutching children, peered fearfully from the tents where they had hidden. They watched us, round-eyed, with their hands to their mouths. Old Flint was among the hunters, staring as we approached. There was a quivering, a drawing back, as if any moment they might all break and run.

Bark trotted beside us. When we came close, my crow, Black, opened his mouth, flapped his wings, and squawked to be fed. I heard a murmur as if a dead person had risen from the ground. The hunters gripped their spears, and cold fear pressed on my heart even though I could see that they had carried home a fat deer.

I reached up and patted Thunder's neck to show them that she would not hurt me. "It is just a horse. I have tamed a horse . . ." I stammered, feeling a little foolish.

Flint nodded weakly. "Do not kill it," he said. "I fell from a tree. The horse carried me home."

Old Flint stared at us for a long time without speaking. I remembered how strong and brave my father had seemed to me when I was small and he returned from the hunt with meat for our hungry bellies. Now he looked shocked and uncertain. Moss saw that Flint was hurt, and a sound like pain came from her lips. Everyone else was silent, staring. Finally Old Flint called Grandmother Touch-Sees.

She alone was not afraid. She came forward, feeling her way with her stick. Then, together, Old Flint and Moss helped my brother down. I could see that my mother was biting her lip in terror. Grandmother carefully felt Flint's leg and touched his head where the blood was.

"It is a leg and a head I can mend," she murmured. Moss began to sob.

Then Grandmother ran her hands over the body of my horse. Thunder trembled a little but stood very still. Her sand-colored coat glowed in the late sun. Bark stood nearby, his tongue hanging out, guarding what belonged to me. Grandmother chuckled. "So this is what you have been up to, Fern. Your mother will surely think you are a witch now!" She stroked the sleekness of Thunder's neck and the softness of her muzzle. She spoke to my horse:

"You I have only heard, these last years, thundering and whinnying across the steppe. I have only touched you cold, to butcher with my flint knife. I like the feel of you warm. You feel strong."

Then she turned and spoke to the others, and her voice did not crack but was full, like a deep pool in the river. "It is my thought that we should keep this horse alive. It may be that the Spirit of Life made it for our use, like the dog who tracks game for us. If a horse can carry home an injured boy, perhaps a horse can carry other things as well."

Some of the hunters scowled. Horse meat is very good. But Grandmother was the oldest person in the *ahne*. They must listen to her. They looked at Bear, the strongest hunter. He nodded. Then slowly my father nodded too. My mother stared at me as if I were some sort of stranger.

I buried my face in Grandmother's robe. Laughing her grass-hen cackle, she stroked my hair. "Perhaps one day your horse will carry Touch-Sees when these old legs get too lazy to walk the earth for themselves."

I looked up to see her lips drawn back, showing her worn teeth and gums in a wide smile.

Chapter Six

SUMMER

We call the season of hot weather *omu*. We also say that a woman is *omu* when she is growing to fullness before the birth of a child. Sometimes, after a big meal, my father rubs his belly and says that he is *omu*. When he has learned a new flint-knapping skill, or Hawk has told an especially exciting story, Old Flint might hold his head and say that his brain is *omu*. We all felt *omu* the summer that Thunder first came to our *ahne*.

Every day we learned something new from my horse. That first evening, while Grandmother, Moss, and Old Sun Dog took care of my brother, my father and I puzzled out how to keep Thunder near the camp. A cluster of people stood near, watching, ready to run if any new magic should happen. Some held darts and throwing sticks ready despite Bear's warning frown, and I heard more than one person mutter about wasting good meat.

"Show me how you make the beast follow you," my father said. When I handed him Thunder's rope, he hesitated. Was Old Flint afraid of my horse? My heart thumped strangely to have my father look to me to learn something.

Suddenly I was shy. "Do not look at her when you ask," I said. "Be like the lead horse of the herd and look where you want her to go. Talk to her with your voice and the rope. Tug here and walk forward. She will come."

In another moment many hands were reaching out to try leading my horse. Thunder began to dance a fear dance and roll her eyes the way a horse does before bolting. Her hind foot stamped twice, as I had seen horses do when they are about to kick. "Please leave her alone—" I started to say to the others, but Bear saw what was happening.

"The girl child speaks for the horse," he said. "The Spirit has chosen her to understand the animal's thoughts. Fern alone shall decide who will touch the horse." That was all he needed to say. The others backed off and watched silently. I saw suspicion and fear in their eyes. I swallowed. It was not heard of for a girl my age to be in charge of any but little brothers and sisters.

"You cannot continue to keep the horse in the gully," my father said to me. "Wolves or a cat will eat her. She must be kept near the safety of our fire."

"Could we build an enclosure?" I asked him.

"It is a long way to drag so many poles, and sometimes we camp where there are no trees at all."

"And she must eat . . ." I said.

For a moment my father was lost inside himself. Then he looked thoughtfully at Thunder's feet. "You have heard of the Night People?" he asked me at last.

My eyes widened, and I shuddered. "Yes."

"The Night People do not honor Earth Mother and Sun Father. They worship a white horse that they keep alive, making sacrifices to it of other horses. They eat no meat except horse flesh. They keep a small herd, slashing the tendons of their hind legs so they cannot escape. When their old white horse dies, they mount its hide, with hooves and head attached, on a pole over their killing place until they capture another."

"The Spirit of Life must sicken at such waste," I whispered. My cheeks burned, remembering the body of

Thunder's mother. I had wasted that by not telling my people. But surely saving Thunder had been worth it. "I would rather give Thunder back to Earth Mother now than to cripple her," I said.

"I was thinking of another way. Maybe we could tie her legs so that she could walk a little—like the crippled horses—to graze, but not run away." He was already working, cutting, twisting, and splicing a stout cord. My father is the best flint knapper and spear maker of our *ahne*. Many others come to him to learn his skills. I felt a thrill of joy to see his hands working for me, for my horse.

Then I had to help my father, who had taken the life spirit of many horses, fit rope hobbles around the feet of a living horse. I made sure I could slip my fingers under the ropes but that they also could not slide off.

We stood back to see what would happen. At first when Thunder tried to walk, the strange things around the fetlock joints of her front legs made her leap, snorting in fear. She pitched forward and fell onto one shoulder. I tried to run to her, but my father grabbed my arm. "She is not hurt," he said. "Wait."

My little horse rested a moment before struggling to her feet. She stood very still, as if thinking. Then she took a few careful steps. She stopped and nosed at the ropes. She snatched a mouthful of grass, looking at me while she chewed. Suddenly there was a shriek of laughter from the camp. Thunder spooked and tried to run again but could not. She stumbled, but this time she did not fall. After a moment she stepped forward slowly. Now she seemed satisfied that she could still hunt her favorite grasses. She did not fight the ropes anymore. Perhaps her time in the bog had taught her patience as well as trust.

I sat with my father, watching Thunder grazing in her hobbles until the others had gone off to their cooking fires. One at a time the fires of our ancestors began to glitter in the sky. Bark crouched in the grass watching her. When, step by step, she drifted too far away, Bark would get up and trot back and forth, his eyes fixed on hers. If she took a single step farther, he would dart forward and snap at her legs. Then Thunder would move back toward the camp, and Bark would settle down to watch once more.

My father shook his head, a look of wonder on his face. We were silent a long time. Then he said to me, "When you were small, only a year or so past your naming, we could not find you one day. Tears ran down your mother's face, and she breathed in gasps. We searched every tent, then turned to the endless steppe.

"It was then that I thought of the horses. In those days you babbled of little else. Remember the horse's tail that you carried about just as Little Brother carries his Wolfie now?"

I nodded, remembering how I loved twining my fingers through the long, glossy strands of hair.

"At that time you saw the world mostly from your mother's back or lap, from behind her legs or under her elbow. You heard many stories in the winter nights, but it was the story of how horses came to be that you loved best. You used to rock back and forth, begging, 'Tell about Hekwos, the Spirit of the Wind. Tell about the horse!'"

Again I nodded, seeing the huge shadows on the pithouse wall as the storyteller's hands moved. The shadows had looked to me like horses running.

My father continued. "I can still see you galloping around on your two little feet, tossing your head, whinnying, and snorting. You threw scraps to the dogs, pointed at every bird or animal you spied, but when you saw horses, you squealed and kicked, crying for me to catch one for you.

"A herd had been grazing within sight of our *ahne* for several days, but we had not hunted them because we had recently killed two bison. I found you behind a clump of feather grass, on your belly, watching the horses, not a spear's throw from a mare and her new foal. It was the first of many times we found you watching the horses.

"Your mother said then that you were touched by darkness, that something was not right with you, that she should not have kept you. We have feared your kinship with animals. . . ." My father looked at me then and touched my face gently. Tears began to fall from my eyes. "Perhaps we were wrong," he said. "Because of this magic of yours, the animals give their powers to you." He sighed. "But it is strange to us and still a little fearful. It is a new path, like the ones our river takes now and then, but we do not know where it will lead."

The next morning I awoke half afraid that Bark had not kept watch all night, but there were horse and dog, grazing and watching, just as we had left them. My brother Flint woke groggy from the strong tea Grandmother had given him and groaning that he was dying from pain. The next moment he remembered my horse and demanded to be helped out to see Thunder.

"Am I not a hunter, now that I have brought home a horse?" he asked our father.

Old Flint snorted. "It was the horse that brought you

home on her shoulders like a bundle of broken roots, young crow." Then my father said something that I could have hugged him for. "For good or bad, the horse belongs to your sister. Never forget that."

That day, and for many days, I lived on Thunder's back, lost in the joy of being part of her running, wandering world. My people whispered and stared after me. I saw mothers pull their children to them when the girl-who-tamed-the-horse rode near, but I did not care. Each moment, it seemed, Thunder and I understood each other better.

Soon she would let Willow and Berry stroke her. They came like nervous birds, fluttering and clucking every time she whooshed air through her nose or swished her tail. But Berry liked her. "You are *tisat*, like sun on the water," she whispered in Thunder's ear.

Of my friends, Berry was my favorite. Her eyes were so exactly like two big, shining blackberries that I was sure that was how she had been named. She could be slow to understand and let herself be pushed around by Willow, but once she was sure of a thing, she stood by it.

Willow hung back. "My mother says that you should be learning to scrape a horse's hide, instead of being carried around on the back of one. She told me to stay away from you." But Willow could not help touching the soft fur of Thunder's muzzle and whispering, "Horse, you *are* beautiful."

As if in answer, Thunder raised her head, ears moving at the sound of dogs barking somewhere down along the bank of the river. I thought that there is nothing so *tisat*, so beautiful, so shining, as the creature that is Horse.

Grandmother said Flint must keep the splint tightly lashed and not put any weight on his leg for at least a moon passage. He took that to mean he did not have to work, although it did not stop him from hopping around one-legged, leaning on a stick, shooting darts, and even swimming with Wing and Cat Feet. When he could walk again, Moss sent us to gather firewood. Flint had tied a bundle together and was lifting it onto his back when he looked at me and said, "Your horse could carry this."

I opened my mouth to say, "You lazy brother, carry your sticks yourself," but then I saw that he was right. We made another bundle the same size and fastened them with rope on either side of Thunder's back. At first she rolled her eyes and snorted. A stick poked her in the haunch, and she jumped sideways. Quickly we unloaded her. We had to start slowly, with just a few pieces at first, but after several days Thunder would carry easily what two of us together might have struggled to lift.

We found that she could drag long sticks behind her from a rope fastened around her shoulders. Then my brother climbed onto the sticks and Thunder dragged him along as well. So it was his laziness that taught us the way that, in time, we would come to move our tents from camp to camp, wandering farther than ever before over the steppe.

Moss helped me weave two large gathering baskets, which we fastened with ropes on either side of Thunder. From the way my mother frowned, I could tell that she was fighting with herself, but she could not hide the fact that she was pleased. "Never before could I get you to sit still long enough to learn how to make a decent basket," she said finally. "You work well when you have a reason."

We put many things in the baskets: dried dung for fuel, roots, water skins, even grinning Little Brother when I was tired of carrying him and my mother did not see. Moss still would not touch my horse or speak her name.

Thunder truly liked to work. When she was dragging firewood, she arched her neck until the muscles bulged. She pulled like the strong waters of the river. I think strength was pleasure to her. And I think she was glad that she and I together had found this purpose for which the Spirit of Life had made her.

As soon as his leg was well, my brother begged me to teach him to ride. I smiled to myself. I could say yes or no, but I chose to say yes. The first time Flint sat on Thunder's back to learn how to ride her, the high bone between her shoulders bumped him between the legs until he hunched over and tears sprang to his eyes.

I could not help it. I laughed. "You must sit back and move with her," I said.

Still he hunched on her neck like a frog clinging to a reed, bouncing against her. When he tried to make her run, Thunder spoke against the bumping on her back by lowering her head and tossing him into a patch of weeds. These broke his fall, so his weak leg was not hurt, but my brother rose up yelling because they were nettles and his skin burned all over. Grandmother made a paste of comfrey leaves and rubbed it on him.

Flint drew his eyebrows together. "Make your horse carry me!" he demanded.

"Do not be rude to her by hurting her back," I answered. "If you want her to carry you, you must move with her like the river water when it glides over the sand, not crash against her as it does on the rocks."

Flint still scowled, but he tried again. After that it was better. Soon my brother, too, heard the wind whistle in his ears the way a diving eagle must, and felt himself riding with the rhythm of flying hooves.

"Remember that she is not a fully grown horse," my father said as he watched us working with Thunder. Then he said, almost to himself, "Ah, but if she is this strong now, how will she be in a year's time?"

Sometimes the herds came near. Long before we felt the ground shake from their passing, Thunder would lift her head and call to them. There were many words that came into being with the coming of Thunder. One of these was *bridle*. When she was in her rope bridle, working for us, I did not worry that she would run to the other horses, but I always kept her hobbled when I left her. Then she browsed lazily along the riverbank, swishing her tail at flies, but the moment I slipped her bridle on and leaped onto her back, she wanted to fly over the ground with me. Black had found his wings now and skimmed along in the air after us, shrieking crow screams of excitement. Bark, too, loved running. We were not girl, horse, dog, and crow then, so much as one flying spirit of joy.

By summer's end Flint could ride almost as well as I could. The other people of our *ahne* saw the things that Thunder did for us. People began to look at me and even smile again, and the men began to talk of how we could get more horses. How to capture one alive without hurting it was a puzzle.

But the salmon had begun to run, and we had to dry much fish for winter. Then it would be time to harvest grain and move to the *b'ahut.*

Chapter Seven

Badger

The last fish had hardly been put away before the hot sun of midday was followed by the first freezing night. The endless winds that pour over the land changed from a steady flow to a stinging torrent. It was time for all the *ahnes* to come together to our cluster of pit houses that lay against a south-facing bluff where the river bends away to the northwest. This was our cold-weather home. It was called the *b'ahut*, which is the same word we use for a hand clenched into a fist.

The move always took several trips, with each person carrying as much as he or she could manage. Flint and I placed Thunder's baskets on her back, filled with packets of dried fish, roots, and berries. We fastened two long poles over the baskets. When we had lashed crosspieces to these and tied on as many of our belongings as Thunder could pull, we stopped.

Little Brother climbed onto the load and bounced a little, saying, "I be carried."

Old Flint, my brother, and I looked at each other in amazement. Moss said nothing, but I felt sure she was glad not to have to carry so much. By herself the young horse could pull as much as our entire family could carry. We could make the move in one trip if we liked.

"We will come back and help the others," Old Flint said.

"Thunder could carry you, Grandmother!" said my brother.

Grandmother cackled and shook her head. "These old legs still like to walk," she answered. "I may ride when you have taught that big, hard-footed puppy not to toss people into the nettles."

When we came within sight of the *b'ahut*, we saw that we were the first *ahne* to return. The cluster of empty pit houses looked lonely, but soon, I knew, smoke would rise from each vent hole, and there would be the sounds of voices, laughter, and dogs barking. Flint and I, with all the other children, ran, dropping our burdens helter-skelter, everyone to their own house. Ours was on the east side, because Moss liked to see Sun Father come up over the dark winter steppe, to make her smile even in the cold. I looked around eagerly. Even though I hated to see the days of summer wandering end, it was good to be home.

Wolves, foxes, and vultures had cleaned the trash thrown into the hollows of abandoned houses until nothing was left but bleached bones. There was the great fire pit in the center of the *b'ahut* where we celebrated feasts and hardened our clay cooking pots. There, circled by a fringe of golden barley with full, nodding heads, was the hard, bare threshing ground where we trampled and winnowed the winter's grain.

I raced Flint. A marmot had been using the roof of our house as a sunning place. It squealed in surprise and scuttled away. Dried grass and weeds had blown inside and collected in corners. I swept a mat of it from a sleeping bench with my hands, and a jerboa and her nest full of babies exploded in my face, making me squeak as loudly as they did.

"You will have to go back to your own *b'ahut*," I scolded. "This is our house." I stretched out in my old sleeping place and, with a finger, traced the pictures that I had drawn on the wall with charcoal and ochre. There were eagles, fish, deer, and bison, but mostly there were horses: horses running, horses grazing, horses kicking and playing. I had not known, when I drew them, that one day I would tame one for my own. "I claim my old bench!" I said.

"I claim this one," answered my brother, flopping onto the opposite bench and looking up at the sky through a place where the summer winds had torn a hole in the roof. "There! The Spirit is showing me a sky bison," he said, pointing to a billowing gray cloud that really did look like a bison galloping with its head down across the sky. "Soon I will kill my first game and become a hunter."

I smiled. The cloud-bison was a good sign.

Suddenly there was a hoarse cawing sound, and the bright eye of my crow, Black, peered down at us through the hole in the roof. He picked at the crumbling clay with his strong beak and dropped a piece onto Flint's head.

"Ow!" my brother yelled, rubbing his ear, but he was laughing at the same time.

"Come inside—this is our winter nest," I called to Black. He squawked at us some more, but he hated dark places and would not come. Instead Bark, hoping that it was him I had called, rushed through the doorway and leaped upon me. I pushed him down and outside again. "I am sorry, friend of my heart, but Moss would be angry to see you coming into the house. Remember, this is your sleeping place out here by the doorway."

I went back inside, lifted the flat stones covering our storage pit, and found Moss's cooking pots and grinding stones stacked neatly there. In summer we carried only one grinding stone and a pot or two with us. As I crouched by the hearth, I could almost smell a good meat stew bubbling.

"Look, here is Little Brother's clay dog you made," said Flint, who had actually begun cleaning out his own sleeping place. "Do you think he will remember it?" Almost at the same time, we jumped up and dashed back out to the others.

"Your pots are unbroken!" I called to Moss.

"Look what I found!" Flint put the clay dog into Little Brother's hands. He grinned, turning it over and over.

Moss tried to smile. I knew how she hated the coming of winter. I took her hand and tugged her onward. "The barley by the threshing ground is fat and bursting," I said to her. "It will be a good winter."

"Help your grandmother," she said to me. "She is very tired."

◦ ◦ ◦ ◦ ◦

It was near dark when the first of the other *ahnes* approached the *b'ahut.* People saw me leading Thunder back up from the river, where I had taken her for a drink after her long day of pulling loads. She was tired and walked beside me like a big, friendly dog. The hunters gave a shout, and several raised their spear throwers and set their darts. "Get away from the horse," one called to me.

But my father and brother were ready for them. "Do not shoot! It is a tame horse," they called back, stepping between us.

"A tame horse?" *Tame* was not a word we used often—once in a while for a dog, but that was all. "Tame?" they whispered to one another. Children came running for a closer look, then stopped short a safe distance away. Dogs barked and howled. People forgot the usual greetings and stared. Snow, the leader of this *ahne*, and the other hunters came to see my horse. The brown, weathered faces of the men showed nothing, but I could see glints of fear and amazement in their eyes. I stood very straight. Thunder trembled a little, but I held her bridle tightly and whispered to her, "They will not hurt you."

Then Bear told them about how I had brought Thunder to our *ahne*, and Flint and I rode for them. We showed how we could gallop and turn and stop, how we could leap off, clutching a handful of her mane, run along at her side, and leap back on again. We showed how we fastened her carrying baskets on her back with straps, how we hitched her to poles to drag a load.

One by one the other *ahnes* straggled in. In the next few days, as we prepared for the cold time, people chattered together excitedly, greeting each other and sharing news of the summer, but mostly the talk was of my horse. Many people wanted to touch her, lead her, try riding, but others shook their heads and looked fearfully at her or stared at me with wary eyes.

The women swept out the houses. Then we pulled down the tightly rolled bundles of winter sleeping robes and clothing, which had been hung from roof poles out of reach of foxes and other gnawing creatures. We unrolled them and spread them in the sun and air.

Flint and I seized our winter tunics as soon as they were unpacked, for with the coming of cold nights, we had begun to shiver in our summer clothing. But Flint could not get his tunic down over his shoulders. We had to peel it off him like a snakeskin.

"My son has grown into a young bear," said Moss proudly. Grandmother took the tunic and began to slice the seams open. She would sew wide gussets into it so that it could be worn another season. Mine was tight as well but needed less adjustment. It stunk of mouse urine, and an exposed edge had been chewed.

Moss stroked the worn fringe of fur around the opening of the hood. "I do not suppose your father could be so lucky as to kill a wolverine this winter." No fur is as valuable, for it sheds the ice of our breathing, so a face encircled by wolverine fur is always warm and dry. But no animal is as evil tempered and hard to kill.

"Wolverine?" asked Little Brother, his eyes bright with excitement.

"It is a creature that is all slashing teeth and claw, held together with sinew and hatred," Flint told him. "One of them can steal all the catch from a string of snares, then drag away an entire haunch of venison to its lair, all in one night. It will defend its thievings with glittering eyes, horrible snarls, and strength like a devil."

Then Moss held up Little Brother's tunic from last winter. We all laughed. "It looks like a shirt for a doll," I said. So much work in all those tiny stitches—and the beautiful little black-tipped ermine tails sewn onto the shoulders! But other mothers were unrolling winter clothing and finding the same problem. Soon they began to gather by the great fire pit to trade outgrown tunics, leggings, hats, boots, and mittens that could not easily be altered. Others sewed their love for their children into their garments as well. Moss returned with a beautiful little suit of wolf fur that Singer's son had outgrown. Little Brother squealed and hugged it.

"We ought to sew your Wolfie-tail right to your bottom, and then when you wear it, you can *be* Wolfie," I said to him.

"You are too big for that old thing," Moss said, trying to take Wolfie from him, but he fought her fiercely until she gave it up. "He will still need new underclothing," Moss said to Grandmother, slipping the tunic over his head to see how it fit.

Moss had traded Flint's old boots for a fine pair that Wing could no longer wear. "I think I have enough wool saved to stuff them freshly to make new linings," she told him. For me she had been able to trade for a soft inner shirt with little wear and a good pair of mittens. "Try not to let that dog tug on these and destroy them as you did your old ones," she said. "They might have lasted another winter."

The men mixed clay from the riverbank with dried grass and set about patching roofs. Thunder helped drag firewood from the nearby *kolki*. People were amazed at how much work she could do. We children strapped her pack baskets over her back and took her out collecting dried dung for the winter fires. The *kolki* are far apart on the steppe. Fuel is precious.

That night the men gathered by the great fire pit and spoke of how they might capture and tame more young horses. I felt proud but also uncomfortable. People whispered and stared at me. Berry and Willow sat giggling with some other girls with their backs turned to me. Every now and then the new girls looked over and stared, so I knew my friends were telling them all about how strange I was. "I have seen her eating grass, just like a horse!" I heard Willow tell them. Berry was only following her, but that did not make it hurt any less. I wished I could be invisible, like the wind, so I slipped away to talk to Thunder and Bark.

Bark showed me another family of jerboas in the grass. I busied myself making a house for two of the half-grown babies in an old, cracked pot. Little Brother was as happy as I was to hold the friendly little creatures and watch them eat seeds, while I cupped my hands over his to make sure he did not drop them. When they got bigger, they would be able to climb up and chew through the screen of twigs I wove for a cover, but still it would be fun to keep them for a while.

When I rose the next morning, I found the pot lying broken outside and my mother's eyes following me as she silently tended the morning fire.

"Why did you do that?" I demanded.

"You will *not* teach Little Brother this animal magic," she said.

"It is no magic! It is only listening and seeing what the Spirit has made. Animals are friends!"

"Great or small, they are meat that devours us if we do not devour it first."

She turned back to her work, and I could only stare after her as if she were a stranger.

My mother continued to ignore Thunder and all the wonderful things she could do. It seemed we were always angry at each other. "You should be stitching your marriage tunic with the other girls," she scolded, "instead of spending all your time on that animal's back."

I shrugged. "I do not want to be married."

"Your clothing is covered with horse fur and you stink of horse sweat. Anytime now you could begin your blood cycles. What man would want a girl who thinks she is half horse?"

"There is no better smell than horse smell. Leave me alone!" I shouted.

Thunder helped with the barley harvesting, patiently carrying her baskets for us. She was happy, fattening herself with snatched mouthfuls of grain. It seemed right that she should have a share. Black stuffed his crop as well and carried off grain to hide in places known only to himself. We had to chase away other crows and flocks of sparrows that descended in clouds on the fat heads of grain. A single sparrow might carry off only a few seeds, but many birds together could steal much. Despite my hopeful words to my mother, we had seen better harvests. But if the hunting was good, it would not be a hungry winter.

The winds blew colder. Day and night the sky was filled with geese and ducks, headed south. We gazed up at them hungrily. It was like the running of salmon. Sometimes they landed in the rushes at the river's edge to rest and feed, and when they did, the hunters trudged home with fat birds to sizzle over the coals. The cold would come now. Whether our storage pits were filled to bursting or not, it was time for the Feast of *Omu.*

Willow and Berry had been sewing for months ahead of time so that they could wear their finest clothing for the feast. We scorned the boys in our own *ahne.* Sometimes a marriage came about after the Feast of *Omu*. But I had sewn nothing at all.

"Maybe the horse-girl is not really a girl at all," Willow said when I would not sit and sew with them.

She put her hand over her mouth and whispered something to Berry, who looked up at me quickly, then down again, her cheeks flaming.

"What did you say?" a tall girl named Reed asked, leaning toward them.

Willow whispered it to her. Reed giggled. Then she looked at me and said boldly, "Willow says you like animals better than you like boys. I say, too bad your horse is a female or you could mate with it!"

I opened my mouth to say something sharp, but nothing would come out. I hated them! They were all such empty-headed grass hens, cooing and preening if a boy were near and then picking on anyone who did not join with them.

I still could not think of boys my age as anything more than trouble. They were just like my brother. Who could love big-footed, smelly creatures who ate like wolves and used their sleeves to blow their noses? Sometimes I made waking dreams about Wing's older brother, Antler, who sent shivers down through my belly if he passed near me, but I knew that he was too old for me, and besides, he would soon be married.

The night before the feast, I took a piece of a deer's shoulder blade from the refuse pile, brought it to the fire, and began carving a comb.

My brother laughed. "Fern seeks a husband at the feast! Toss it in the fire, and see if you can see his symbol in the cracks that Fire Spirit draws on the bone."

I ignored him.

He tried again. "Snow's baby son would make a fine husband for you if he lives through the winter."

Moss frowned at him. "Hush—do not be so foolish. And of course he will live through the winter," she said. Her eyes glanced toward Little Brother, who sat by the fire sprinkling crumbled clay into an old basket and stirring it with a stick.

When my comb was finished, it was heavy and thick. Again Flint teased me. "You might untangle thistle down with such a fine comb!"

I was silent.

Flint said, "I am sorry. I did not see that your hair has grown matted like a horse's tail. That is it. You must be going to comb a horse's tail with that war club of a comb!"

"That is exactly what I am going to do, you buzzing fly," I said.

Flint looked at me, amazed.

"Thunder must look her best for the feast."

Moss stared at me and sighed. "Do you not care at all how *you* look, Fern? Who ever thought of combing a horse?"

"I did," I said.

She muttered, "The Spirit punishes me for saving you," and turned away.

My eyes stung at her words. Well, I could not be what she wanted me to be. The Spirit had given me Thunder. I could not turn that gift away any more than I could change the fact that I lived and my mother was sorry for it.

At daybreak Flint helped me pluck burrs from Thunder's hair. We combed her all over. I had to use a blade on some of the worst mats, but after much work the hairs of her tail flowed softly through my fingers. "You are a pretty girl," I whispered to her. Then I plaited a few late flowers that had not been killed by the frost into her tail, while Flint rubbed goose fat onto her hooves to make them shine. Thunder butted her head against my arm. She knew she was beautiful.

Later that day I stood with my filled bowl, wondering where to sit. Not with the women or men, not with the boys, and *not* with the girls, I said to myself. But if I sat completely alone, everyone would stare at me. Reluctantly, I found a place just outside the group of chattering girls and began to eat.

I looked up to see a boy named Badger watching me. The mouthful of juicy venison suddenly tasted like dirt.

I knew who he was. He was the son of Grass Fire, the leader of the largest *ahne*, who was said to be the most skillful marksman with the spear thrower. Badger was fourteen and had killed a small aurochs bull by himself that year. He wore its dried testicles on a piece of gut around his neck. He was big, and the muscles across his shoulders bulged and rippled as he walked, but his eyes were small, like the eyes of a bear, and mean. Now I saw that when Badger looked at me, the corners of his mouth were smiling, but his eyes passed over me like I was a bundle of trade goods.

Later, as I was passing behind one of the pit houses of the *b'ahut*, hard hands suddenly gripped my arms. Badger's voice hissed into my ear. "You are almost a woman. It is fitting that the son of the greatest hunter should marry the girl who tamed the horse. My father will speak to yours."

Then he pressed his mouth, which smelled like he never cleaned it, against mine and squeezed the tender places where my breasts were beginning to grow. I fought, but he was too strong for me. He laughed. This was no fight with my brother. Then a shadow lunged from behind him and Badger let go of me to clutch his thigh, cursing. Bark stood between us, growling, head low, stiff legged, the fur on his shoulders standing up like grass against the wind.

I rubbed my mouth until my lip split, then ran crying to Grandmother, but I would not tell her what had happened. Putting it into words would make it real, the way a storyteller makes the happenings of our lives into a thing that cannot be lost as long as we have tongues to pass it along. I thought I could forget it if I did not tell, but I could not forget.

Chapter Eight

HUNGER

The next morning, while I was filling my bowl with gruel, my mother turned to me with a smile of pride on her face. "The son of Grass Fire has spoken to your father. Old Flint told him that when you begin your blood cycles, we will let him know."

I dropped my bowl on the hearthstone, breaking it in pieces. "No!" I said. My stomach flooded with sickness.

Moss looked at me in surprise. "It would be a fine marriage. He is a strong young man and has already made his first kill."

I felt dizzy. "He is filthy. He smells like dead meat."

My mother laughed. "You and your children would never go hungry."

"Hungry?" I asked, leaping to my feet. "Do you think I care if I am not hungry if I have to live with a pig? I would rather marry a man I love and starve."

"You do not know real hunger," she said to me then in a low voice, staring into the fire. "I would not have you know it."

I looked at Grandmother, who sat in silence, working a small deer hide back and forth over the teeth of an upside-down horse skull to soften it. She seemed not to have heard anything we had said. I ran outside and whistled for my dog and my horse.

Black flapped down to roost on Thunder's withers. She had grown used to him now. Her skin twitched a little when she felt his claws, but she did not toss him off. He stalked up and down along my horse's back, muttering to himself, sometimes stopping to tug at my earring or a strand of hair, while I cried into the fur of Thunder's neck. Bark pressed his head against my leg. Why did people have to talk about marriage and husbands now? I was not ready. I was still a girl. I did not want to be a woman! Then together my animal friends and I wandered far over the steppe, until those beasts, hunger and cold, drove me back to my home.

◦ ◦ ◦ ◦ ◦

Winter was easy at first. I did not need to hobble Thunder unless the herd of wild horses was near. She found enough to eat pawing through the snow within sight of the *b'ahut.* Bark still brought her back if she wandered too far, and now she would come to my whistle, for I always had a handful of grain or dried berries for her when she came.

We had games. Whenever I went outside, Bark demanded to play mitten, tugging on one until he yanked it off my hand in triumph, then scampering like a puppy while I chased him, shaking it as if he were killing a marmot, or tossing it in the air and catching it again with a loud snap of his teeth. I felt guilty about the tooth marks on my new mittens, but I could not say no to such joy.

When Thunder heard my whistle, her head would come up from the grass and her ears prick forward. Her game was to come toward me slowly at first, then break into a trot; and finally her hooves would make their thunder, drumming on the frozen earth as she galloped straight for me, with maybe a buck or two thrown up if the wind was brisk and cold. I would stand like a tree, and she would stop short in front of me, nostrils flaring, feet dancing, to bury her muzzle in my hand, her soft lips and tongue seeking and finding each morsel of grain. My thank-you was always an impatient shove of her head, as if I were a grain pouch to be butted and spilled onto the ground.

"Easy, my little greedy one," I would say, laughing. I was as full of love and pride for my horse as a mother is for her child. What did I care if people thought I was strange?

But as winter grew old, it also grew more bitter. The hunting was poor. The herds seemed to have been swallowed up by the snows. Old Sun Dog seldom left his fire. He spent his days chanting over bones in the coals and peering at the cracks that appeared in them to learn where the game had gone and why the Spirit of Life was keeping them from us. He burned herbs and drank potions so that his spirit might leave his body and go wandering over the steppe searching for these answers.

Yet day after day the hunters went out and returned with only a grass hen or two, or a hare. They began to mutter and look sideways at my horse. "Tell them she is worth more to us alive!" I begged my father.

"I have done that," he said, "but the time may come when that is no longer true."

I could not slip any more handfuls of grain to Thunder, but still she came to my whistle, for she loved scratching and combing and the soft sound of my voice as well. Her body did not miss the treats. She was round just from eating dried grass. She had filled out and was beginning to look like a grown horse now. It was good, riding her in the cold, feeling her shaggy warmth against my legs or pulling off my mittens to bury aching-cold fingers in the heat of her fur.

Bark and Black also had to hunt for themselves. Sometimes Bark would be gone overnight running with the other dogs. Sometimes he came back with a torn ear or some other new battle wound, but I knew he would always come back. I felt sure also that some of next spring's puppies would be handsome and friendly like my dog.

Now Black, too, disappeared on hunting trips for long spells. When I spotted a lone crow winging toward the *b'ahut,* I would whistle long and shrill. In another few moments he would spin down out of the sky to land on the roof of our pit house, cackling, fluffing his glossy feathers, and blinking his wise eyes. Then he might fly to the ground and pace over the packed snow between the houses, talking crossly to himself and looking for mice or bits of food.

But our stores were almost gone and there was little or no fresh meat. Everyone's belly began to moan with hunger. My clothes felt loose on my body. When Flint undressed by the fire one night, I saw that his shoulder blades jutted out.

The hungry time continued, and now I noticed that people's faces had changed. Berry's and Willow's eyes no longer curved into merry crescents of laughter. They were big and ringed with blue shadows. Their full, ruddy cheeks had shrunken to yellow skin stretched over bone. I put a hand to my own cheek. My face must look the same.

On a glittering cold afternoon, Badger threw down four grass hens, tied together by their feet, at our doorway. My mother seized them up with a cry of joy.

"Here is meat," he said to us. "Until Young Flint becomes a hunter like me, I may bring you more from time to time." He cast an appraising eye on my horse as she grazed nearby, and his knuckles clenched upon the haft of his spear thrower. "I wonder why people are hungry when there is a fat winter feast grazing so near. I can kill it with one dart if you say the word." Then he looked at me. My face burned, but I would not look back. Bark growled a low rumble, warning of danger. I crouched beside my dog and put my arm around him. Through his thick, shaggy fur, I felt ribs. He was hungry too.

My brother Flint scowled. Without saying anything, he stalked off with a fist full of snares. We fed well that night. I swallowed my share. Still I did not think that marriage to Badger could ever be worth a full belly.

At breakfast I saw Moss slip a morsel of her own food to Little Brother. Later that day Grandmother did the same thing. My mouth watered, but I was glad for Little Brother. Sometimes I would save a scrap for the times when he would whimper and come begging from one to the other of us, but mostly I was too greedy, and my portion disappeared into my own belly before I could remember to force myself to save some for him.

That evening Grandmother tried to give her portion of food to Little Brother, but Old Flint put his hand over hers. "Eat it, old mother," he said.

Grandmother said quietly, "I was thinking perhaps it was time for me to take the Walk of the Old Ones."

"No, Mother!" cried Moss.

"We have much need of your knowledge," said my father. "We cannot spare you."

Later my father squatted by the fire, charring and straightening arrow-wood shafts for darts, working them through a hole in a horse's jawbone. Each dart was nearly as long as he was tall. They were hard and light and would fly true. He worked points, carefully flaking the edges with an antler tine, until they were deadly sharp. He fletched his darts with eagle feathers if he had them, but mostly with goose feathers. As I watched, his hands stopped in their work and he stared at the fire a moment. Then, without looking at me, he said, "If we do not kill anything on this hunt, we must butcher your horse, Fern."

I cried soundlessly until I finally slept from exhaustion, for I knew he was right.

On the third day that the hunters were gone, Flint brought home a single hare that Bark had chased to him. He had stunned it with a lucky throw of his thong and stones. I say lucky because my brother was not a good shot. He captured most of his game with snares.

"There was another," he whispered to me, "but that greedy dog of yours caught and gobbled it before I could get it from him."

"Bark must eat too," I hissed.

When the hare was roasted, Flint and I wolfed our bits, leaving the bones on the grinding stone for Moss to pound and boil into soup. Then we slipped silently back outside. Flint left to check and reset his snares.

I called Thunder and rode her to a place where the river begins to drop down out of the steppe land. I gathered green pine needles from a few scraggly trees that I found there. I chewed on a lump of spruce pitch for its flavor, even if it could not fill my belly. Black flew down along the river and returned with the skeleton and head of a small sturgeon, which he pecked at from the top of the pine. Like a bear I dug and hacked with a small hand axe at some rotten limbs that lay on the ground and was able to collect a handful of grubs to put in my carrying pouch. Bark helped me with the digging. I did not like them raw, but I ate some anyway, sharing them with my dog. In a gully I found a few shriveled apples and bird cherries still on the naked branches of the trees and tucked them in my pouch as well. The river ran down between some boulders, and on them I discovered big, gray curling lichens. I had come much farther on Thunder's back than I could have on foot. When I returned, Moss was pleased.

"I can go farther to look for food on Thunder's back," I said. "So even if the hunters come home with no meat, we do not have to kill her." Bark wagged his tail as if he were proud of the grubs he had helped to find.

Moss smiled a small smile. "What you brought is good. Your grandmother's gums bleed, and dried fruit and pine needle tea will cure it, but boiled lichen and pine needles are starvation food. A horse could feed all the families of the *b'ahut* for several days." Then she added softly, "You might capture another in the spring."

My miserable stomach thought of great juicy hunks of roasted horse meat and growled. Then dizziness came over me and I ran outside, retching yellow stomach bile into the snow. Flint was just returning, empty-handed. Seeing me, Thunder lifted her muzzle from the snowy grass and nickered as if she would gladly take me on her back again. I felt such a pain in my chest, I could not speak. Thunder was not just any horse now, wandering the steppe at will. Like Bark, she was my friend. How could we kill and eat her?

"We have to find some other meat," I said to Flint. My twin gathered his spear thrower, a fistful of darts, and his stout javelin with its harpoon point. From atop Thunder's back each of us scanned the white world that lay all around us, squinting against the sun on the snow. Was there anything alive, any living thing of flesh and hot blood in this world of bitter cold? Bark trotted ahead of us, his tail over his back.

Three times my brother shot at, and missed, hares that burst from snowy hiding places to zigzag away from us.

"Let me try it!" I said, angry when his dart went wide the third time.

"No!" he shouted. His belly ached as much as mine, but his pride as a male must have hurt him more. I had never heard him sound so fierce.

Then suddenly Flint, who rode behind me, grabbed my shoulder and pointed. A lone bison cow and half-grown calf had appeared, like creatures made of smoke, along the horizon. "But the hunters have not returned, and I cannot stalk them alone," he said hopelessly to me.

"Thunder can outrun a bison," I said to him. "From her back you could spear one."

"And eels can dance," he said with a snort. "How could I ride and throw at the same time? I have not yet been on a hunt. I do not even know if I have the strength to kill a bison."

The creatures were so close now that we could make out their shining eyes under shaggy brows. "The calf could trade his flesh for that of Thunder," I pleaded. I knew that I could ride better, but he was stronger.

Flint stared at me a moment, and I saw his eyes grow hopeful. "I can try," he said. "But you and Bark must run on foot and head them off." I slid to the ground. My dog and I began our long run to get ahead of the bison so that they would have to turn toward the river and be cornered. Quickly Flint set his darts and throwing stick upright in the snow, where he would be able to find them again. Then, taking only his javelin, he urged Thunder forward.

Almost instantly the cow spotted them. She snorted and broke into a heavy gallop, throwing clods of snow and grass up behind her. The calf stayed beside her like a shadow. Wind seared my eyes until they watered as I jogged with my head turned, watching Thunder stretch herself out flat. She was running for joy. Bison are not *tisat* as horses are when they gallop, but they can move fast. Still, slowly but surely, my horse overtook the calf. Flint raised his spear.

"Now!" I screamed. The word was torn from my mouth by the snarling wind. I wondered if he could hear me screeching encouragement. Could he ride and throw at the same time? I saw Flint push Thunder closer with his leg. His face seemed like the mask of a person I did not know. His lips were curled back from his teeth like a wolf's. Then he let go of Thunder's mane and, with both hands, drove his spear downward. I could not see what happened in the flurry of snow and animal legs, but clearly across the distance between us, I heard my brother's javelin snap. The calf scrambled to its feet and fled to its mother. My brother was still on the horse.

Flint was gasping for breath as he rode back to me. Thunder's coat was dark with sweat. Steam made clouds around her body as she walked. "It is no use—it cannot be done," he said brokenly. "I was a chattering squirrel to think it, and now I have shattered my best spear." He leaned along Thunder's hot, wet neck. I too pressed my face into Thunder's neck, smelling her good smell through my tears. I felt dizzy and weak after running with so little food in me. If the hunters returned without game, this might be our last time together.

Then I saw something move at the edge of my sight. I turned my head, and my insides lurched. There, where the steppe swelled into a ridge, like the backbone of some great animal, stood the returning hunting party. Their shoulders sagged, but it was with weariness only, not the weight of meat. Thunder rubbed her head against me as the hunters approached. Several of the men gripped their spears as if they were only too eager to plunge them into my horse's side.

My brother's eyes met mine, and his mouth was twisted in pain as he slipped off Thunder's back and faced our father. "There were two bison," he said to Old Flint, "a lone cow and calf. They went that way." He handed me Thunder's rein and then just stood there, staring at his feet.

Old Flint looked past us and said softly, "It would be dark before we could get close to them. The only way to hunt a lone bison is with many hunters running in turns until it tires. Even then the hunt is not always successful.

We have not fed well in many days. A hunter cannot run far on an empty belly."

I knew what must be coming then, but I did not want my father to be the one to say it. Instead I made a picture in my head of Little Brother looking up at me with eyes like a baby hare, his little bare buttocks as shrunken as those of an old man, whimpering for food. I held out Thunder's rein to Old Flint.

"My little brother is hungry. Here is meat," I whispered. I was so dizzy, I thought I would fall.

Old Flint stared from one to the other of us. The muscles in his face worked, showing many thoughts. Then it seemed as if something flashed in his eyes. "It is a good offer, Daughter, but from the ridge I saw a hunter-not-yet-grown fly after a bison—faster than a man can run—on the back of a horse. I saw him *nearly* make his kill." He turned to Flint. "Even hunters miss their target sometimes, my son, but until your aim and strength are surer, you must wait."

Then he turned to the others with a short laugh. "The Spirit has given us yet another use for this horse, but our eyes have been to the ground, following the ways we have always traveled. It has taken younger eyes than ours to see it. Do any of you have the strength to make a chase while the bison are yet in sight?"

Several of the younger men stepped forward, Badger among them, his eyes fastened on me, willing me to choose him. They all looked to me to see what I would say.

I felt my face grow hot. Most of them had tried riding Thunder, but Antler was lightly built and had ridden her more than the others. He would not hurt her. So what if Badger was angry? I indicated that Antler should ride.

Badger spat into the snow and glared at me. Squatting in a circle, the men gnawed at some of the last precious bits of smoked meat from their traveling pouches. Then Antler, followed by four others trudging behind, my father included, rode Thunder away toward where the cow and calf were now small smudges in the distance. Badger turned to stare back at me, and the ugly expression on his face made the hair rise up on the back of my neck.

Before the sun went down and the white steppe turned the blue-gray color of a falcon's wing, they returned, staggering with exhaustion. Beside them Thunder plodded steadily forward, dragging the carcass of the cow. The hunters carried quarters of the calf on their shoulders. Antler walked at Thunder's side, his face shining with triumph.

My hands flew to my mouth. I closed my eyes and

thanked the Spirit of Life. My horse could live! She was more valuable to us than ever. Because of her we all would live.

They had not yet reached the outer circle of the *b'ahut* and the rejoicing people of our *ahne* when I ran forward, slashed off a chunk of meat with my knife, skewered it, plunged it into the coals a few moments, and thrust it, on its stick, hot and juicy, into Little Brother's hands.

Chapter Nine

Apart

My mouth watered as the meat was divided. The dogs had to be kicked back. They'd had the entrails as soon as the bison were gutted, but they could not help wanting more. Even my crow dashed in and out, dodging humans and dogs, to steal what he could. Dogs snapped at him, and one nearly caught him by the tail. Bark, too, could hardly control himself.

A gray male dog leaped forward and snatched a stray hunk of meat. Instantly two others fell upon him, and the three became a whirling, snarling mass of teeth and fur. Hawk broke them apart with a firebrand. Amid laughter, yelps, and the stink of burning fur, two dogs slunk back, but the third, a large white male, paused to swallow the stolen meat in three ravenous gulps before backing away.

I felt sorry for the gray one, but nothing could be wasted. The dogs could lick blood from the snow and snuffle after scraps and hide scrapings, but we could not give them even the bones until we had split out all the marrow and boiled as much goodness as we could from them.

With nearly two tens of families in the *b'ahut*, it was not easy to divide the meat. The shares had to be different because each family had different needs. Raven and Brook had only Antler and Wing, but Antler was a hunter and Wing would be one soon. Young men eat much, and hunters must be kept strong, for they are our weapons against hunger. Wolf and his new wife, Singer, had many at their fire: the three children of Wolf's first wife, who had died, Star Grass, Runner, and Painted Sky, as well as their new little ones, three-winters-old Lark and their unnamed Little Brother, plus Wolf's father, Old Sun Dog—so many bellies, but most of them small.

Finally it was done. I found myself snatching at raw bits as Old Flint carried our share inside. We all picked and gnawed on snippets as it cooked, laughing when we burned our fingers and mouths. Nothing had ever tasted so good to me as that hot meat juice and melting fat on my tongue. Moss was watchful to see that we did not cramp our shrunken bellies. She boiled some meat broth for us to sip slowly and fill us, then carefully put away the remainder to ration until there should be another kill. I'd never seen my father so tired. Almost before he swallowed his last mouthful of broth, his eyes were closed.

Little Brother finished his meal by suckling at Moss's nearly dry breasts until he fell into a happy sleep. This was his second winter. After his third, we could celebrate his Naming Day. I wondered what name would be chosen. I wanted so much for him to have his own name, but it was too soon to think of that. I closed my eyes and felt strength and happiness flowing back into my body.

Later that night, when all had eaten and rested awhile, we heard the *thump-thump-thada-thump* of Bear's reindeer-skin drum calling us outside. Each family left its cozy home fire and crept out to stand, wrapped in sleeping robes, in the space between our pit houses, where a fire had been built. None of the houses was large enough to hold us all, so we gathered here. The snow under our feet was packed hard, and our breath rose up to the glittering stars of the frozen night.

Why had we been called? Antler had been a hunter

for two seasons, so there was no need for a ceremony. But it was, indeed, a first-kill ceremony, though brief because all were weary and it was bitter cold. Still, a first-kill ceremony must be made before the spirit of the animal has traveled too far to share the honor of it. Bear stepped into the middle of the circle and strode slowly around the fire, turning as he went, so that his voice reached all of us. "Because of the horse, Thunder, we eat tonight. She became the legs of the hunter, Antler. It is her first kill. Although a beast and a female, she, too, is a hunter now."

Then Bear motioned to me and put the cutting teeth of the bison cow into my hands to give to my horse.

Hawk began to sing the Song of the New Hunter:

Body, mind, heart
Joined together
As flint, sinew, wood.
Only to eat,
Only to live.
Life gives life.
Honor the hunter.
Honor the spirit of the life given.

I looked at my brother and saw the fire glittering in his eyes. I knew how much he was wishing for his own first-kill ceremony. Overhead the stars were more brilliant than on the brightest summer night. There were so many, each one the hearth fire of one of our ancestors. I wondered that so many people could have walked to the spirit world in all the yesterdays behind us. Perhaps, I thought, in the far world of many tomorrows, the night sky would be so filled with the fires of the dead that it would shimmer as bright as day. Suddenly a star flashed and fell down across the sky to the east. It seemed to me like an omen that soon the Song of the New Hunter would be sung for my brother.

I lay awake that night, listening to the breathing of my family all around me. In the dark above me, the smoke hole was filled with stars that moved in their paths across the night sky. My good dog and crow slept in their places guarding our doorway, and my shaggy little horse slept, standing with her tail to the wind, nearby.

The next day I carefully drilled a hole in each bison tooth. My father helped me, so I did not break many drill points in the work. This took much time. "You are learning patience," he said. I looked at him with gratitude and suddenly had to brush water from my eyes. If only Moss would just once speak so to me!

I made Thunder her first real bridle then, from good,

strong leather, rubbed well with fat to make it supple. Grandmother helped me with the work. For a girl my age, I was not skilled at the task. At last I was finally showing some interest, but my mother seemed never to notice the care with which I softened and cut the leather strips or the neat holes and stitches that I made.

Now I made a band just long enough to lie flat across Thunder's forehead. One by one, I sewed the teeth onto the band. Then I attached the ends of it to the side pieces of her bridle with tiny stitches, as close and even as I could make. A hunter usually wears the teeth of his first kill about his neck, but this seemed right to me—for without her bridle Thunder hunted only sweet grasses and treats from my hand. Besides, a thong about her neck could easily catch on something and either hurt her or be broken and lost.

Thunder danced a little at the clicking sound of the bison teeth as I put this bridle on her for the first time. I felt pride, but also a tiny sadness. She was a hunter, valuable to the *ahne,* yes, but somehow a little less mine.

In the months that followed, with the help of my horse, we mostly ate well. Sometimes I felt jealous when others asked to ride Thunder, but I could not say no. From Thunder's back the hunters were able to kill and drag home aurochs, bison, even other horses. It seemed traitorous to ask my horse to help kill her brothers and sisters, but we must eat, and our people had always eaten horse.

With Thunder to ride, Flint and I could set snares far apart. Each soft little fur—hare, ermine, fox—was carefully worked and saved to make inner clothing or hats. All of us were cheerful in those last days of winter as the fear of hunger slipped away. Often now as we sat by the fire at night, Grandmother would tell a story, or Moss might sing and Old Flint make music with his bone flute. The words and wandering melodies made pictures in my head so bright that I closed my eyes and lost myself in them. One night Little Brother toddled over to our parents' sleeping bench. He tugged on the edge of the old bearskin that they slept under, looked at Old Flint, and demanded, "Play bear!"

Old Flint smiled. "It is good that you are fat enough again to want to play your favorite game," he said. Then our father got down on all fours, pulled the bearskin over his shoulders, and chased Little Brother around the hearth, clawing the air with his hands and growling, "Arghh arghh rarhhh!" Flint and I helped the game by protecting Little Brother or being extra bears in turns. Little Brother shrieked and dodged away until it got so wild, he was almost crying in pretend terror.

"Enough bear play or my pots will all be broken and little toes burned in the coals!" cried Moss, wiping laughter tears from her eyes. Although it was not spoken of, we all rejoiced that Little Brother would be seeing his second spring. In the entire *b'ahut*, we had lost only three old people and one child, a little girl who had not been strong from her birthing day. In spite of the hungry time we had survived the winter.

Even before the *ahnes* split up for the warm season, there were many attempts made to capture and tame other horses. Horses were driven into the bog. Horses were trapped with rope nooses. Horses were wounded just enough to bring them down but not to kill. Young horses were captured. But none of these could be ridden.

At first I thought that it was because the men were not gentle or patient. Bones of both men and horses were broken, and several horses died. I tried to help, to show them soft touches, whispered words, and handfuls of sweet grass, but these horses seemed different to me. There was a look in their eyes, and almost a smell, I cannot say of what, that told me they were not like my Thunder. One horse, after being tied up, starving, for several days, would eat from my hand, but any time we tried to get on his back, he reared into the air and threw himself over backward. Fear clutched my belly each time I tried to help tame one.

Then one day a young man from Turtle's *ahne,* Stalker, was thrown to the ground and struck his head on a rock. From the moment his head hit, he never moved again. By the time they carried him into his house, his face was blue. I lay awake on my sleeping bench all through the night hearing the wailing of his mother and sisters.

"I will not have you killed," said Moss to Flint and me the next morning. "Leave this horse taming to the hunters." Then she said, without looking at me, "It would be better if you do not get on the back of any horse again."

My head snapped around, staring at her wide-eyed. *Not ride Thunder?* "The other horses act out of fear. I do not know why it is, but Thunder is different. She is not afraid of people. She would never hurt me on purpose!"

"But she is big. She is a prey animal who must sometimes run without thought in order to stay alive. You could still be hurt," my mother said, low.

I looked to Old Flint. "Father," I pleaded, "now that I have known what it is to ride, I would rather do that and perhaps sometimes be hurt than live the rest of my life on the ground."

Old Flint looked uncomfortable. He did not answer me. I had seen his pain each time Moss lost a little one—pain as much for her as the child. Tears were streaming down my face now. I pointed angrily at my brother. "He will soon be a hunter. You will have to let go of him then. I suppose he will get to gallop with my horse while you keep me safe at your side like a suckling baby!"

I felt my grandmother's fingers seeking and then clutching my arm. "Hush child," she said. Then she spoke to Moss. "A bird that cannot fly becomes dead inside. The Spirit of Life has chosen your daughter to ride this horse. Hekwos watches over them. It is her right to ride. I think it is true that this horse, Thunder, is not like the others. Perhaps the Spirit has chosen her to be a friend to our people. See how much she has done for us already. We must not turn such a gift away."

My mother's eyes met mine, and I could see that the pain in them was as if her flesh had been torn, but it was she who dropped her eyes first. "Do it if you must then, but it is not a thing in which I can ever take joy. Perhaps I have already lost you. Perhaps I was never meant to have you."

I did something I had not done in almost a year. I put my arms around her and whispered, "I will try to be careful."

My mother stiffened, saying nothing.

Why do you not hug me back? I wanted to shout at her. *Do you not love me?*

No one could deny the usefulness of Thunder, yet Stalker's death sent me back into a world apart from the rest of my people. It was accepted now that my horse was indeed different, that other horses could not be tamed. Grandmother, my brother, and my father believed as I did, that Thunder was a sweet and good gift to us, that perhaps somewhere there were other horses with a kind nature like hers. Other people like my mother said that being carried on the back of a horse was crazy and unnatural. There were whispers of magic and witchcraft. Always now I was aware of eyes avoiding mine, of exchanged glances and stares.

Chapter Ten

Skyfire

The world grew warm again, but I was happy only when I was with my horse. Then I could escape the shadow of Badger, my mother's sad eyes, my friends who no longer seemed like friends, and the uneasy faces of those who distrusted me. With Thunder I could truly feel like myself.

Soon I would be a woman. Maybe I would have to go as a wife to some young man whom I did not love. It would *not* be Badger. The thought made my stomach turn. I would run away first. I would sooner face the vastness of the steppe alone with my dog, my horse, and my crow than be with him.

Early that spring, when the snow had not yet disappeared, my crow flew away from me. At first I could not believe it when dusk came and his roost remained empty. "How can he just leave like that?" I asked. "I thought he was my friend."

Grandmother chuckled. "Perhaps he has found another friend, Fern. It could be possible that a beautiful young woman crow has snared him."

My mouth opened and then closed in surprise. I had not thought of that. But a nest full of baby Blacks would be good to think of when I missed my bright-eyed friend. Then I thought of something else. "Grandmother," I said, "how do we know Black is a boy and not a girl? Remember how he loves *tisat* things? How he stole Moss's shell hairpin?"

"Yes, but males love beautiful things too. No one loves to strut about wearing a thick, glossy bearskin more than a man. With some birds it is easy to tell, but I do not know how it is with crows."

"But why do we call Little Brother's Wolfie a boy? It seems that everything is male unless we know different."

Grandmother was silent a moment. Then she said, "It has something to do with males being stronger. The hunter is the chief of the family because he brings meat."

"But there would be no hunters if it were not for

women," I answered angrily, "and my father seldom does a thing if my mother is against it."

Grandmother smiled, "Ah, now you are learning the secrets of the world, Fern. Women are the givers of life, patient, enduring. We have our own ways of ordering things—sometimes through love, sometimes through means less honorable, if it is necessary."

It was my turn to be silent, pondering her words—*if it is necessary*. Then Grandmother must believe that there were times when a woman might be right and the man wrong, and that she must try somehow to change things.

All my life I had felt jealous of Flint because he was male and would someday be a hunter. Oh, I could remember Grandmother stitching a long gash from a bear's claw on my father's thigh, his groans of pain, the fever as it festered but finally healed. Then I was glad I would not grow up to be a hunter. Still, it was clear to me that my brother was somehow better because he was male.

He was talked about proudly, how he would be strong and his fame sung around the fire. He was given more food and choice morsels. I, on the other hand, could look forward to marriage to a man who smelled like a refuse pit and a lifetime of drudgery, keeping his hearth. But worst of all was feeling that no one would ever listen to *my* thoughts, that *my* name would never be spoken of by others with honor and respect.

"Grandmother," I said low, "I would like to have my name spoken of by the fire, as a hunter does—and I want to marry a man like my father, a man who will listen to my words, a man I can love. My mother thinks it is only important to be fed."

"Fern, your mother has suffered much, both starvation and losing babies. Somehow her thoughts were blackened."

"I think," I said very slowly, considering the meaning of each word as it came, "that men and women should be different, because that is how the Spirit of Life made us, but we should each have the same value."

Grandmother Touch-Sees smiled, and her smile seemed a little sad. "You will become a wise woman someday, I think, but things change very slowly. It has been this way since very long ago. You must not let your anger spoil your joy in life or your friendship with men. It is good to work. When you have babies you will find that you will do any amount of work gladly for them. As long as the man works in his way, equally hard, it does not matter what work either of you do—or whose name is spoken of by the fire. But I, too, would have you marry a man you can love and who will honor your thoughts."

For many days I looked for Black every time a flock of crows flew over the *b'ahut.* The sky was terribly empty without his wild cawing in response to my whistle. I blew through my lips until they were dry, but no bundle of black feathers swooped down to land, croaking and clucking like an old man, tugging at my braids and earrings, ruffling his feathers and pacing back and forth on my shoulders.

Then one morning, after I had given up hope of ever seeing him again, I stepped outside and he was simply there, perched on our roof! He was ravenous, talking excitedly, like five crows instead of one, and puffed up over his adventure. When at last he let me stroke his feathers, he crooned as if he were a baby again, saying, *Urrrrlll urrrlll urrrlll,* dipping his head, and tugging gently at my finger with his great adze of a beak.

I snatched some chunks of meat out of the cooking pot, blowing to cool them. Black danced with impatience as he waited to bolt them down.

After that Black no longer lived with us all the time. Often he was gone for days, to return when I least expected him, for he knew that where Fern was, a lazy crow could always find a meal. Sometimes I would whistle for him when a flock of crows was near, and a speck would break off from the rest to come circling back to me, and it would be Black.

Willow, Berry, and the other girls and women spent much time now gathering shed winter fur where it clung to twigs and bushes. They made felt by fluffing and wetting the fur, rolling it in a fresh hide, and beating it until it was compacted and flat. Felt hats shed wind and rain, and felted vests were very warm. Felt mats on the floor, if one could find enough fur, made a pit house snug.

In the afternoons the girls sat in the warm sunshine gossiping and sewing beads onto their marriage tunics, which they had already begun. But for me there was no other life than the world from the back of my horse. I did not want to think of the future.

Then it was time to roll up our winter bedding and clothes for storage once more. I wondered if I would wear my winter tunic another year. The leather was shiny and worn at the elbows, but it was still not too small. There had been no wolverine killed to replace the trim around the hood. My body had changed a little, but I had not grown much taller. My boots still fit as well. Maybe by the next cold season I would have a woman's shape and need a beautiful new tunic. Then I remembered Badger.

My mouth turned sour, and I wished I could always stay a girl.

Grandmother had suffered during the hungry times of the winter, yet I did not think she had aged greatly. She still scolded Flint and me with much energy when we fought, and no one could skin a hare, cut it up, and put it in the stewpot quicker than she. Nevertheless, when it came time to close up the pit house and travel to the fish camp, she made a show of the stiffness and pain in her knees. When all was ready, she whispered something in Little Brother's ear, and he took her hand and led her hobbling to Thunder's side. With great ceremony, she announced: "The horse, Thunder, who is friend to the People of the Earth, will carry these tired old legs to the fishing place."

Moss scowled, but Flint and I lifted her up onto Thunder's back. I showed Grandmother how to grip Thunder's mane for balance. She closed her blind old eyes and turned her face up to the sun, feeling its warmth.

"Grandmother, I am sorry that you can no longer walk," I whispered to her.

"I can walk as well as ever I could before, young vixen," she snapped back at me. "I just thought it was time to know what this riding upon the back of a horse is like. Your mother ought to try it."

I knew that other families were watching us with interest. People respected my grandmother. She was showing them that she trusted my horse. "Thank you, Grandmother," I whispered.

One day my brother and I rode far to the east along the river. Suddenly Thunder stopped and tossed her head. A shrill whinny echoed from the high steppe to the north of us. A herd of horses was not far off. Thunder trembled and danced sideways. Her winter coat had shed, short and slick, to a bright sand color that glinted in the sun. Flint, hunting with his spear beside us on foot, went to her head to calm her.

"No, Thunder, you belong to us now. Let them go," he said.

My little horse stamped and plunged. The pounding of hooves echoed off the rocks around us as the wild herd made its way down to the river.

And then the stallion was there, frozen in charcoal and ochre, exactly like one of the drawings I had made on the wall in the pit house. The only movement was the wind ruffling his short, upright mane and lifted tail.

It seemed that sparks flashed from his amber eyes like the fire spears thrown from thunderclouds. In that moment I gave him a name, Skyfire. His nostrils flared, and he stared at us like a hunter who knows that he is stronger than all others. Suddenly the stallion switched his tail and snorted. He flexed the powerful muscles in his neck and began advancing toward Thunder.

"Quick, Flint, get back on!"

I stretched out a hand, and my brother swung up behind me. With all my strength I pulled Thunder's head around and beat my heels into her sides until she raced away. I turned my head in time to see the stallion wheel and gallop back to his herd.

"You will have to check her hobbles carefully at night and guard her closely by day or you will lose her," said Old Flint when we told him about it. "The mating urge is strong."

I stared into the fire. How could I keep the stallion from stealing Thunder?

I was awakened next morning by a harsh cawing. Flint turned over and grumbled in his sleep. Bark pushed his wet nose under the edge of the tent, first into my face and then into my brother's. Quickly I rose and slipped out to feed fish scraps to my crow to shush him. I smiled. Black was a beggar and a thief, but sometimes a good friend for spying trouble and reporting it loudly. He did a stiff-legged dance now, wings arched, pinion feathers quivering. *Urrrl urrrl kak kak kak.* It was his little crow chant of expectation. For a moment he allowed me to stroke his head, blinking his pale-blue eyelids. Then I gave him the fish. He wolfed it in great hunks until he could hold no more, snatched the remainder, and flew off to hide it. As I watched him go, my thoughts were deep.

That afternoon, as I was doing the same old miserable springtime work of helping Moss and Grandmother hang fish on racks to dry in the sun, the stallion came near the camp with his herd. All the women and older children were busy at the task, while little ones splashed along the gravel spit in the river and babies snoozed on their mothers' backs. My brother was just coming up from the river with a fresh basket of fish.

Long before we could hear any rumble of hooves, Black began to cackle and then caw loudly, dancing and flapping along a branch in his excitement. Thunder lifted her head from her grazing and stamped restlessly, nostrils working and ears pricked. Then I heard the first whinny. Quickly I slipped to her side, looped a rope around her neck, and secured her to a stout little willow tree. I do not know why I was so foolish, but many times now I had tied Thunder by her neck, and she'd come to accept it without fuss.

A dust cloud appeared out along the track that hooves had used ever since the Spirit made the first horse. They galloped—as many horses as all of my fingers counted three times over—a surging mass of muscle, hide, and dust. The stallion bellowed. Thunder called back to him in a voice that sent a shiver down my spine.

Then she stood on her hind legs and did what I had not imagined she would ever do. She fought the rope until the whites of her eyes showed and every vein on her body stood out. Grandmother sat back on her heels motionless, watching with everything but her eyes. Moss clutched Little Brother to her breast and screamed at me. Thunder was on her haunches now, barely breathing.

"Give me your knife!" I turned to my brother and snatched at the flint knife in its sheath at his waist. Mine was lying on a rock ten paces away.

"No! We will never get her back—you cannot let her go!"

I shook my brother, trying to wrest the knife from him. "She will die now, or break her legs in her hobbles some night. And for a horse, that is as good as dying."

Now Flint saw that I was right. He took out the knife

himself, tears streaming down his face, and cut Thunder free.

My little horse stumbled sideways, regained her feet, and stood a moment, sides heaving. Then suddenly she picked up her head, whinnied, and without once looking back at us, galloped after the herd.

My brother flung his knife into the sand and turned away, shoulders hunched. I reached out a hand to him.

"She will come back," I said. "She is our friend. Remember, Black flew off to the other crows in the early spring and then returned, cackling and crooning, as happy as Grandmother Touch-Sees when Little Brother was born. And Bark sometimes slips away in the night when the wild dogs are singing and comes home in the dawn, hungry and wagging all over to see us again."

The dust had settled and the pounding of hooves was gone. Once more we heard the sounds of laughter and splashing from the river and quiet talk among the women. I stared into the empty distance where the river wound away into the shimmering grasslands. My chest hurt so much, I could scarcely breathe. Thunder could not leave me forever. She would not.

"She will come back," I promised my brother. But my heart was not so sure.

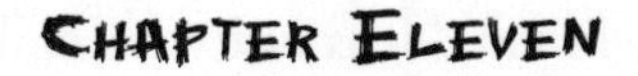

EMPTY

Usually I thought of spring as a time of softness, of flower petals and sweet smells. In winter the wind sometimes made my cheeks feel as if they had been slapped. The touch of the warm spring air flowing over the steppes was how I thought a kiss might feel. But now I found that there could be harshness in spring too.

In the *kolki* sharp green sprouts pierced their way through the wet brown leaves of the past season. Our river rose, jammed with breaking ice, to surge in a fury of brown water. All through that season there was an emptiness in me that made the sweetness of the days cut like the edge of a knife. Everything reminded me of my horse: the new grass, an eagle's cry, even the strong, fresh wind itself.

Bark felt it too, and often looked out over the empty grassland and whined. "It is not your fault," I told him, stroking his head. "Someday she will come back to us."

My brother spent many days searching for Thunder with me. He did not want her back only because of the things she could do for us. I knew he had come to love her too. If we chased her back into the bog, could we get her out again now that she was full-grown? We had tried and, with the help of Bark, had actually cut her away from the herd once. But we could not run fast enough to keep her headed in the right direction. The stallion had overtaken her, slashed with his teeth at her flanks, and driven her back to his family.

"What if we dug a pit, as the men do to trap game?"

I rolled my eyes at my brother. We had been talking by the fire after the evening meal. Most of what we talked about was Thunder and how to get her back. "And she would be broken like a fallen tree," I said. "You have seen the hunters trying to capture horses alive. Horses do not come out of pits and still run."

"What about a snare? We could bait it with apples—"

"She would panic and hurt herself. No, we must wait. I think she will come back on her own." But we had spent many long days tracking the herd, and still Thunder did not return.

There was an anger rising inside my brother these days too. For long spaces of time he would throw spears with the other boys, both the long darts with the throwing stick and the javelin, but his aim was poor. He was sure that someone had let his darts get wet so that they had dried crooked, the fletching was coming loose, or the weight of his spear thrower was out of balance.

I was as swift a runner as any of the girls, and I could lug two full water skins up from the river like a grown woman now, but my brother could run faster still, carry more, and—what had made me most envious—leap onto Thunder's back more easily than I. Yet he thought himself puny and half blind.

One day I watched when Old Flint tried to help him. I liked to toss the long darts with the throwing stick. It was good to see them fly farther than my arm alone could send them. "Let me try," I said. After several of my darts sang truly into the target, my brother scowled and said, "Why do you waste time here? You would make yourself a more valuable bride if you learned women's doings."

I wrinkled my nose. "The women are busy working hides. If scraping rancid fat and gristle all day makes me valuable, I would rather not marry."

Old Flint smiled. "It is not a bad thing for a woman to shoot well," he said to my brother. "Your mother prefers the more traditional women's duties, but when your grandmother was young, she could knock a low-flying duck out of the sky even on a windy day. There have been times when her skill was needed."

I bugged my eyes at my brother. "See?" I said.

"But Daughter, the soft, white saiga skin that you like so much does not appear in our hands as a gift from Earth Mother. The gift is the knowledge and patience for working the leather."

"I can make good leather," I said. "Thunder's bridle is as soft and strong as living flesh." Then I closed my eyes to hold back the tears, because Thunder's bridle was lying unused next to my sleeping place, carefully wrapped up in my best shirt.

My father put a hand on my shoulder. "Yes, I have seen you spend much time working leather straps for your horse, but a grown person learns that some work must be done even if it is not what we wish most to do."

My brother set a dart, bounced lightly on the balls of his feet, and flung his arm forward. The dart struck the dirt three paces wide of the target. Its long shaft shivered in the silence that followed the throw.

"It is always to the same side," Old Flint muttered. "Do you not see that? Try it again."

This time the dart head buried itself deep in the end of the log, still an arm's length wide of where the target was fixed.

"If you know it will stray to one side, you must try to aim more to the other," said Old Flint in a voice that sounded as if he were talking to a young child.

"You don't have to tell me that!" Flint almost shouted. Once again he flung a dart. This one skidded over the log and into the grass behind it, yet again wide of the mark. None of us said a word. Furiously, my brother walked forward to pick up his darts. He knew better, but rather than gently work the point that was buried out of the log, he wrenched it sideways and it snapped.

"You know how long a journey it is to the gravel bank where that flint is found!" growled our father. "A hunter does not waste such material."

"I am cursed like Squinter." The man he spoke of had eyes so weak that he could not hunt or do close work. "I may as well cut myself a stick and feel my way around the world as Grandmother does," Flint said. "Can she brew me a tea for strong eyes and muscles?"

"Only time can turn your body into a man's," Old Flint answered with a smile.

"You eat enough; maybe doing your share collecting dung for the fire and fetching water would help," I said, dodging the elbow he shoved at me.

Old Flint said, "I think your eyes are sharp. You did not miss you mother's hiding place for seedcakes, and you were the first to spot the returning geese."

Flint turned away. "A whole year ago, the Spirit showed me a cloud bison and promised me my first kill. I cannot wait longer. I will die before I am a hunter."

"I do not think you will die," said Old Flint, grinning widely now. "Your mother has buried a sturgeon under the coals, and very soon it will be sending up a magical steam that will bring my son back to life." Then he added, "A boy who is bursting with impatience sometimes shoots spears like an old, blind grandmother. It takes more than desire to become a hunter. You must also learn patience. The spear must fly from your hand like a thought from your lips. The spear must know where it will go as it leaves the hunter's hand. Someday your life will depend on that. Shoot until you can tear a still target to shreds. Then shoot a moving target until you can do the same. Shoot until hand, eye, spear, and thought are one." Old Flint's words were like an old, old song.

There was a silence. Then my brother said low, "Do

you not think I have practiced my throwing as much as that?"

Frowning, Old Flint picked up the pieces of the broken spear point and put them into his pouch. "Well, I can rework these," he said. Then he seemed to remember something. "Look to the great rock by the river," he said to my brother. "You look too, Fern."

"There is nothing there, just the rock," I said.

Old Flint smiled. "Good," he said. "Now each of you hold up a thumb at arm's length and move it until it is between the rock and your eye."

We did as he said.

"Now close your right eye," he said.

"Huh!" I said.

"What happened, Fern?"

"My eye saw my thumb jump to the right."

"What about you, Flint?"

"My thumb did not jump."

"Try it again, but now close the left eye."

"Now it jumps, but to the left," he said.

"But mine did not."

"Are you sure?"

We tried it again. My thumb jumped when I closed my right eye. Flint's thumb jumped when he closed his left. "What does it mean?" I asked.

"Each person has a stronger eye as well as a stronger arm. Usually they are both on the same side. Flint's right arm is the stronger, but his right eye is not. His left eye wants to do more of the seeing. That is why his spears always fly to the side."

"Then I will tear out my left eye and make the right eye see!" said my brother.

Old Flint laughed. "You do not need to do that. Your grandfather had the same problem. At first he tried to learn to throw with his left hand. Some can do it, but for him it was no good. Then he tried closing his left eye. Sometimes he used a strip of leather to cover the eye. That was better, but not so good for moving targets. Yet it helped him to train his weak eye to be strong even with the left eye open."

Quietly my brother got up, gathered his throwing stick, darts, and javelin from where they lay scattered on the ground, and turned back toward the target.

Thunder had still not come back. I did my share of fish gutting, root digging, and berry picking. I helped with setting up, taking down, and moving our shelter. Moving camp was so much work without my horse. The other girls tried to talk to me, but I barely heard what they said.

Flint's anger fell on one place only now, and that was the target made from a worn-out sleeping robe stuffed with dried grass. He made himself an eye cover to wear. When I was fetching water with Willow and Berry, they told me that he looked handsome that way. *My brother handsome?* I squinched up my face as if I'd been eating green fruit and laughed.

Flint seemed to hold himself straighter now. He was not so angry, yet there was an impatience about him that reminded me of Thunder when she wanted to gallop and I wished her to walk. Old Flint took him on a two-day hunt. Wing came home carrying a quarter of the red deer they had killed, and they sang about him that night, but Flint's hands were empty. "I had no good shot," he said to me, although I had not asked.

CHAPTER TWELVE

ROPE

"That is Thunder right over there." Flint's voice was tense with excitement. He flexed his legs, stiffened from crouching. I nodded, scanning the herd of horses that grazed in scattered groups. All were the color of dried grass, but one glowed like golden sand in the odd light cast by the gathering storm. Her tail looked a little less tangled than the others, her coat a little less shaggy. There was something familiar about the line of her head, the strong slope of her shoulders, and the shape of her hindquarters. It had to be Thunder. If she would only turn toward us so that I could see the white marking.

I put my fingers to my mouth and whistled. She

raised her head in response and turned in our direction. The eagle wings flashed in the sun.

"Yes!"

I clutched the coiled rope in my hand. Would she come to us? Thunder had been with the wild herd for much time now. Had she forgotten my touch and friendship? What if deep down she *was* like all the other horses and could never really trust humans? *No*, I told myself. *Thunder is different. She does not fear me. No matter what, she is my friend.*

If she would not come, could we sneak up on her and catch her with the rope? I did not know, but we had to try. Bark whined. I held my hand over his muzzle until he understood he must be quiet. Now my brother reached for the pouch of sour green apples at his belt. "Try to get closer," he whispered.

"Wait. I want to watch a little longer. I want to see if the old mare will let that colt back into the herd."

I pointed to a mare whose rounded belly spoke of many foals. The stallion skirted the herd, always watching for danger, but she decided when and where they would move. I smiled to myself. It was just the same as when my father quietly asked my mother if she thought the barley was ripe, then, when she said yes, loudly ordered the rest of us to begin rolling up sleeping furs, as if it had all been his idea.

The old mare was disciplining one of the yearlings. He had kicked a filly his own age and bitten a skinny old mare. When he bullied one of the new foals, the lead mare turned on him and knocked him down until he retreated in disgrace.

Now he was scared. Alone, he could not fight the big cats or wolves that sometimes stalk horses, hoping for stragglers like himself. He wanted to rejoin the herd, but she would not allow it. Time and again he approached, only to be turned away as she faced him squarely and stared him down. Up he would trot, to be pushed away again by the wise old mare.

Then, as I watched, his whole attitude changed. His head went down; he looked sideways at her, working his mouth like a baby. "I think he is saying he will follow her rules if only she will allow him back," I whispered to Flint. "That is what she was looking for." The mare turned her shoulder to the yearling, and he sidled back into the group. In a few moments she was fussing over him, nibbling and grooming his neck.

"He had to beg to come back before she would allow it. See, they have their own language. Every motion means something."

"Come on," urged Flint. "Thunder has not moved.

We can get closer if we crawl behind those bushes." Hearts pounding, we slipped up to within a spear's throw of her. Bark crawled on his belly, eyes fixed on our little horse. Flint took two apples from his pouch and rolled them along the ground toward Thunder. Her head went up.

"Thunder," I whispered, creeping forward a step or so.

My horse trembled but did not move.

Flint rolled another apple. "Here Thunder, it is your favorite. We found them this morning."

She took a hesitant step in our direction. Nervously she snatched up an apple and chewed, ears working all the time. I talked quietly to her. "Remember me? Remember galloping by the river and getting your tail combed and your itches scratched?"

She finished the apple, enjoying the sweet-sour juice of the fruit. She put her head down for another. I thought that maybe I could walk up to her now, but suddenly Flint burst out from behind the bushes and flung the rope over her head. Bark lunged, snapping at her heels. Thunder threw up her head and pulled against the rope. Her feet drummed the earth.

"Easy girl, easy," I said. I put my hand up to Thunder's neck and rubbed her crest as if I were a lead mare myself, soothing a young one. She quieted and butted my arm. But at that moment there was an angry bellow, and the stallion surged after us. Thunder stood on her hind feet then and pulled the rope so that it burned its way across my brother's palms and slipped out of his grasp. She was gone with the herd again.

"Oh, you knows-nothing brother, in another moment I could have caught her quietly and we could have slipped away!"

The words tumbled out before I saw the sorrow in his eyes, so I did not blame him when he answered, "All right, knows-all-things sister, catch her yourself."

I found comfrey leaves and bound Flint's hands. "Never mind," I said. "She remembers us. She will come back when she is ready." Overhead the clouds were churning, and hot wind suddenly slapped our hair across our cheeks. Bark tucked his tail, whined, and looked at us anxiously. I measured the coming storm with my eyes. "We have stayed too long. We will not make it back to camp. We must shelter somewhere."

"Thunder will snag herself on the trailing rope and be strangled," groaned Flint.

"We will follow them," I answered. "See?" I pointed to her bridle wrapped around my waist. "We still have this. I tell you, Thunder will come to us soon."

The herd moved together now, like spawning salmon. The lead mare headed purposefully toward the blotted-out sun, head down into the wind. A flaming spear of yellow skyfire flung itself out of the sky and a booming crash shook the earth. I could not hold back a scream. Nothing is as fearful as the fire that shoots from the sky. Sometimes it strikes a creature or human. Few survive, and on the steppe there are not many places to hide. I clutched my brother's arm, looking wildly around for shelter as rain began to plaster our wind-whipped hair to our scalps.

"Look," I said to Flint. "The horses have a path down to the river. There must be shelter down there. The lead mare knows, and the stallion is making the others follow." Sure enough, as I spoke the herd plunged into a gully hidden by a clump of scrubby pines.

"Come on!" Flint yelled. We ran over the hard ground with the storm all around us. Panting, we scrambled after them.

"We cannot stay here," he gasped. "Water could come down hard and fast through this place and drown us." We worked our way down and out into a thicket of small trees so dense, it shed most of the rain.

My brother and I hunkered under a tangle of brush

until the storm spent itself. Sun suddenly glittered through dripping leaves, and steam rose from the wet, dark bodies of the horses sheltering in the woods. After a while the herd moved out into the flatland along the river's edge. We followed quietly. Every now and then Thunder turned her head to look at us, but each time she did, I flicked the reins of her bridle at her and she moved off with the others again. The mood of the horses was different now. Two foals with legs like saplings reared and tussled playfully with each other, then, bucking and crow-hopping, cantered back to their dams.

The stallion trotted protectively beside Thunder. Suddenly she snorted, and the two were off in a joyous race along the sandy bank of the river. I caught my breath to watch.

"If only you could draw *that* on the wall by your sleeping place," Flint whispered in an awed voice.

The two horses turned, squealing and bucking, and pounded even faster back to the herd, shoulder to shoulder, wet hides gleaming.

"Look!" I said. Against the dark body of the retreating storm clouds, a rainbow arched across the sky. My spirit seemed to leap out of me for a moment, soaring and singing with the shimmer of the colors. Suddenly I felt very small. Sun Father had shown us this thing of beauty that marks the end of a storm. "Thank you," I murmured. It was a good sign.

The two horses touched noses briefly. Then the stallion trotted off to a small rise. He turned his face into the wind, guarding his herd and ignoring Thunder.

My horse looked at me, her sides heaving. Again I flicked the reins of the bridle at her, pushing her away. She seemed puzzled and anxious now, and I smiled to myself. I could almost hear her thinking: *Do you not want me? Are we not friends? I have been missing apples and soft talk, and I have itchy places to be scratched. Can you not see I am ready to let you leap on my back and gallop with me once again?*

Thunder dropped her head and began a chewing-and-licking motion with her mouth just as the wayward colt had done. I smiled in a curve like the colors in the sky. I pretended I was the old lead mare. I dropped my eyes and turned my shoulder to my horse. Step by cautious step, Thunder moved to my side.

Then, just as I had many times before, I slipped the bridle over her ears. I took Flint's rope from around her neck and breathed a silent thanks to the Spirit of Life that my horse had not stepped on the end of it while galloping and hurt herself. Grabbing a fistful of mane, I swung lightly onto Thunder's back and reached a hand down to help Flint up.

"Come on, Brother, it is time to go home."

Chapter Thirteen

HUNTERS

The cold time came again. One morning in early winter, Flint and I rode to the *kolki* south of the *b'ahut* to check our snares. Some beast had been stealing from us. Often we would find our snares torn apart, leaving only blood and a few fluffs of fur. The days had been sunny, melting the tracks so that we could not tell what creature had been there. This day seemed luckier. Already two large hares were tied by their feet across Thunder's withers. Bark loped happily beside us.

"I want to set a snare in that grove of birch trees," my brother said. "We have not tried that place before."

"Then I will go to the pines beyond and dig for

snowberries," I answered.

He slid to the ground and started into the wood. I was just turning Thunder's head to go when I heard Flint whistle softly to me. I slipped down and led my horse quietly forward. I saw Bark standing like a stone dog with the ridge of fur along his spine bristling. The growl that came from his throat was like no other sound I had heard him make before. Then I saw ahead a tangle of brush and winter-killed birch trees with pig tramplings all around it in the snow. The tracks were huge, showing clearly the prints of long dewclaws. Everywhere the snow was darkened with dung and urine. I took a step backward.

Flint grabbed my arm and would not let go. I thought how unfair it was that we should be the same age, but his arm should be so much stronger than mine. "It is the nesting place of a great boar," my brother whispered, as if I could not see that already for myself. "You must tie Thunder and follow behind with the spear."

"I am not a hunter's spear carrier to back him up when all his darts are thrown!" I said, near panic. "That is a very big boar, and we may both be gored with his tusks and killed."

Flint looked at me coldly. "The Spirit has not shown

me this place without a reason."

"But what if you miss and I am not strong enough to make a good thrust?"

"I will not miss. You will hold the spear only to keep it safe. You say you do not like woman things. Here is your chance to learn to hunt."

Numbly, I tied Thunder to a tree and followed my brother. He had changed into another creature. He was not a boy now, but a silent, stalking thing. I did not exist to him. I could see his nostrils working, seeking the faint reek of the boar, trying to find where the odor was strongest. Bark's nose worked too, tasting the air, searching out the enemy.

The hollow where the boar slept was empty. His body had left a great pit in the snow and earth. I shuddered, wondering if even at this very moment he might charge us from behind. I tried to step as silently as my brother. He turned, pointing out to me places under a clump of hazel bushes where the animal had been rooting for nuts. Then he slipped his fingers into the loops of his throwing stick and fitted a dart in place. "We will wait here," he whispered.

I knew how to go inside myself and become part of the woodland or the open steppe. I had done it many times watching the horse herds. I had to hold Bark by the scruff of his neck, with my other hand on his nose to tell him to keep silent. He shook with excitement. Much time went by. The shadows grew blue and long. Every now and then I could hear Thunder stamp or snort from behind us. I willed her to be quiet.

Then suddenly Thunder screamed. The air was filled with snarling. There was a wild hammering as her hooves pounded the frozen ground. When we got to her, a black, shaggy beast was clinging to her shoulders, ripping at the carcasses of the hares that were tied there. Even as we ran to her, the wolverine began tearing at my horse in fury.

Nothing is as powerful for its size as this beast that we sometimes call slinking bear. One could bring down a full-grown reindeer. I screamed as Bark leaped at the creature. It lashed around in midair like an animal made of skyfire. Dog and wolverine rolled together on the ground. Even though he was larger, Bark was no match for this demon animal. Flint's spear was in my hand, but I was frozen with terror that I might hit my dog if I threw it. Instead I beat at the back of the wolverine with the butt end until suddenly it whipped its ugly head around to lunge at me, teeth bared, little eyes like cold death.

My arms went up to protect my face. I heard a soft

whistle like a breath, and a thud. The wolverine's snarl turned to a shrieking gurgle. I opened my eyes to see it writhing, pinned to the ground with a dart through its neck. It took two more of Flint's darts to kill it, but finally it lay still, its teeth clenched in a hideous grin.

I expected Flint to shout then, perhaps pound his chest and shake his spear thrower at the sky, for a boy who has killed a wolverine is a man in anyone's eyes. But he did none of these things. Instead he crouched to examine the cuts on Bark's face and along his rib cage with gentle fingers.

"You are a hunter," I said to him in a shocked voice, as if we did not both know it.

He looked up at me. "You are not hurt?"

"No. Are Bark's wounds deep?"

"Not very. If they do not fester, he will heal. Grandmother will know what to do."

We turned to look at Thunder's wounds. Somehow she had not broken her tether. She trembled like an aspen leaf in the wind. Blood flowed from a gash in her shoulder, making a dark stain on her dun coat, but the muscle was not torn. I bent my head onto her neck and wept like a weak, stupid girl child. "Oh you poor, sweet grass runner. I am so sorry for you."

I felt Flint's hand on my shoulder. "It is not much. It

only looks bad because of the blood. Already it is stopping. She can carry us home. And see, your dog limps, but he is not badly hurt."

I looked at my brother with deep thanks in my eyes, for in another few moments, my dog, my good spirit shadow, one of the best friends of my heart, would surely have died. I, too, could have been killed.

Thunder would not allow us to tie the wolverine across her back. "Well, I can carry it" was all that my brother said, but I could hear the pride, at last, in his voice.

He had just handed up his darts and throwing stick to me, and was hefting the wolverine onto his shoulders, when there was a roaring like ice breaking up in a spring torrent. Flint's javelin stood upright, leaning against my thigh. I turned to see the boar charging out of the hazel bushes. Its eyes glittered red.

Flint dropped the wolverine's carcass and snapped his spear into place in front of him. There was a moment when he waited for the impact of the huge beast and the world seemed frozen in silence. It leaped, taking the point of the weapon deep into its chest—and kept going. Thunder danced sideways, but I, who had only tried it a few times in fun, set a dart and flung it cleanly through the boar's hindquarters. The air was full of its squealing, but it could no longer run. My brother grunted and fell sideways as a slashing tusk grazed his ribs. But I had crippled the boar. Flint finished it by slashing its throat with his knife.

Now we stared at each other in stunned silence.

Then slowly Flint said, "Whatever happens to us in this life, in the time ahead of us, before we go to make our own hearth fires among the stars, we will always be linked by this moment not just as brother and sister and twins, but as hunters who each owe life to the other. . . ."

I bit my lip and nodded. Flint had killed the boar, but he could not have done so without my shot. We had done this together. In killing the two beasts, in saving each other, our spirits were bound together in a way that only hunters know. A strength that had little to do with size or muscle came into my heart at that moment. I knew for the first time that my brother was more than my brother. He was also my friend.

I only came up to his shoulder, yet I stood tall. I put out my hand to him, and he clasped it with both hands the way that hunters and friends do. In a short time we hitched Thunder with a rope to the body of the boar. Then we headed for home, rejoicing.

Chapter Fourteen

Woman

That night when Bear sang the Song of the New Hunter and presented my brother with not only the teeth of the wolverine but also the tusks of the boar, I felt too *omu* with pride and happiness for him to think of myself. Old Flint's face was stone, but his eyes glowed. No one in memory had attained manhood with a double kill of two such dangerous beasts! As Young Flint took his place with the group of hunters, Old Flint put a hand on his shoulder, and my brother and father exchanged a look that I would not forget.

Never again would I doubt my brother's aim. I was awed by his courage and skill. I saw Berry and Willow exchange glances. It would be a lucky girl who won him as a husband.

But my brother's face was clouded. Suddenly he stepped back into the fire circle and said loudly, "I would not have lived to be honored as a hunter tonight were it not for my sister. The boar did not die at once from the spear in its chest. It might well have killed me in its death struggle if Fern had not disabled it so that I could finish it off. If the horse that is a female could be honored as a hunter, then my sister should also be honored."

He locked eyes with mine and held out one of the boar's beautiful curving tusks to me. In the silence that followed I accepted the tusk, closing my trembling fingers tightly around it. *My name had been spoken of at the fire!* But then I stepped back to my place between Moss and Touch-Sees. A woman might hunt, but she could not truly *be* a hunter any more than a hunter could give birth. I found my brother's eyes again and silently thanked him. One such as Badger would never have mentioned my part in the battle.

So it was that my family all had new wolverine fur trim for our winter tunics. The look on my brother's face when our father first pulled his hood up around his cheeks and said, "Ahhh," was worth the terror of the beast's killing.

My old tunic had grown tight across my chest, and it was decided that I must have a new one. Moss and Grandmother helped, but they did not make it for me. As a girl who was nearly a woman, I was expected to make it for myself.

Half of me took joy in the soft deerskin, sewn in two layers—the outside layer to shed the weather, and the inner layer to trap the warmth of my body. I was proud of the fine close stitches I had learned to make from sewing Thunder's bridle. I could hardly believe that the golden flowers of onion-dyed felt, the carved bone fastenings, and the thick, glossy ruff of wolverine fur were for me.

But the other half of me worried that Badger would notice me more. When at last the tunic was finished and I put it on, Grandmother inspected it carefully from top to bottom, then traced her fingertips lightly over my eyes, cheekbones, and nose. "You begin to be a beautiful young woman," she said.

I thought how strange it was that before I'd met Badger, I had looked forward to leaving childhood behind. I had watched as one after another of the older girls tied her hair in the woman's knot as the signal that her body was now able to grow babies and she was thus ready for a husband. It was such a small thing, to twist one's hair up and pin the shining knot in place, but all eyes saw and instantly knew. A girl was looked on differently from that moment when she stepped out of the tent where the Woman's Feast was held, with her eyes cast shyly to the ground. All the world could clearly see that she was now grown.

Only women attended the ritual when the girl's mother washed, dried, and fastened up her hair for the first time. It was followed with a feast, with laughter, tears, secrets, and advice. We all looked forward to that. But it was the moment of stepping out as a woman, with the eyes of the young men—and perhaps those of a special one—fastened on her, that a girl really waited for. Ever since Badger had spoken for me, I thought that I could not face that moment.

"It is good," Grandmother said, as if she knew my doubts. "A woman should be proud that her body has been chosen to carry life."

"Here is where I keep what you will need when your time comes," my mother told me, showing me the sack of soft, dry moss. She no longer needed to gather moss for Little Brother's bottom now that he ran about, made his water outside, and squatted by the refuse pits like the other little boys. She had known I was close to womanhood and had collected moss for me. Then she gathered my loose hair gently in her two hands, twisting it up at the back of my head, the way she and Grandmother wore theirs. "You will look nice when the time comes."

It felt good to have my hair played with, and something inside me ached for my mother's touch, yet I pulled away from her. Fear flooded through me. I did not want to think of being a woman. If Badger saw my hair up, he would know. In that moment I decided that I would not tell my mother when my blood cycles began. If they tried to force me to marry him, I would run away.

Secretly I gathered and dried my own moss, hiding it in a corner under my sleeping bench. My mother spoke often of Badger. "He is fine and strong, and always comes home from the hunt with meat," she said one day, watching him with admiring eyes as he squatted outside his father's house, skinning a beaver. "It takes great patience to kill a beaver in winter, and no fur is warmer. My daughter would sleep warm and be well fed."

"A slinking bear has a lovelier face," I answered.

She turned to my father. "Is not Badger a fine young man? He has been on hunts with you. It is said that he is not only strong but courageous as well."

Old Flint frowned. "That is true, and yet there is a thing I do not quite like about him. He speaks too much of himself, and he gives way to anger easily. There are many other young men."

"He is the son of Grass Fire," my mother said, as if that made him the child of Sun Father himself.

Not very many days later I was out riding Thunder, lost in the thoughts inside my head. I slid down from her back to relieve myself. "Oh Earth Mother, no!" I stared at the place in the snow where the water of my body had melted a pit. There, clearly to be seen against the faint yellow, were several red drops. Blood. I should have known from the ache in my back and the cramping deep in my gut. Now, when I should have felt joy, I felt deadness inside, as if my life were over. I put my arms around Thunder's neck and whispered to her, "I am a woman now. It is our secret. We will keep it as long as possible."

Thunder stamped nervously as I mounted her again, and Bark whined. I looked around me and felt my breath go out of my body. "Oh . . ." I said. The sky to the west was the color of ashes. Snow as thick as white fur was driving before a rising wind. How could I have been so stupid? A winter storm can come down upon us like a ravenous beast, swallowing us in whiteness. A hunting party overtaken by a storm would hunker down and let themselves be buried, sharing each other's travel furs, warmth, and food until it was over and they could see which way to go again. But even so close to home, a lone person with no provisions, like me, could be lost, frozen, to be found in spring—or never.

I called to Bark and urged Thunder forward, but in moments the snow was around us, choking, blinding. I knew terror then. Because I had not kept watch on the sky, I would die in this swirling whiteness, within sight of the *b'ahut*. The wind tore at me, seeping through my clothing until I could no longer hold the reins. But Thunder went steadily forward. She showed no fear, no hesitation about where she was going. I could just barely make out the shape of Bark plodding along in her footsteps, with his nose almost in her tail. Finally I lay down on my horse's neck for her warmth and let her go where she would.

It was then that I learned another thing of magic about a horse. For a long time she walked, while I slept in a kind of cold-sleep. At last she stopped. Bark spoke to me, took hold of my boot with his teeth, and roused me. Through the thickness of the snow I smelled woodsmoke. Then through the spinning flakes, I made out a half-round shape. It was our pit house! I do not understand how a horse finds its way and lives in such weather, but Thunder knew. I slid off her back, whispering my thanks to her for my life, and stumbled inside, out of the storm.

"Earth Mother!" Moss gasped, getting clumsily to her feet as I entered. "We thought the storm had eaten you!" Her eyes were like two black pits of fear.

I almost fell against her. "Thunder carried me back. She knew the way home. Sh-sh-sh-she saved my life," I stammered through chattering teeth as Moss led me to the fireside and began to strip off my frozen clothing. Before she could take off my undergarments, I pulled the sleeping robe from my bed and wrapped myself in it. My mother slapped my cheeks and arms to bring back the warming blood, and I thought perhaps she slapped a little harder than necessary.

"That is not the way I see it," she said bitterly. "Because of that beast you were alone, far from the *b'ahut*, and like a foolish grass hen you were caught by the storm."

Chapter Fifteen

FEVER

Finally a day came when the wind blew warm from the south and the snow in our dooryard turned to muddy slush. It was not spring, but it was the beginning of it. Moss sorted through her stores of worked leather, drew out a beautiful saiga skin, and began cutting it out to make Little Brother's Naming Day shirt. Old Flint smiled when he saw what she was doing. I dug through the clutter under my bed and found the pouch full of snail shells that I had searched for by the river's edge all last summer and saved to decorate it with when the time came. Grandmother sewed the seams with tiny, perfect stitches. When Moss tried it on him, Little Brother grinned like the Moon Child. He thought it was done then and was pleased to have such a fine new shirt. He did not know how special a shirt it was, that there were many long sessions of work still to be done decorating it.

My mother still said little, and least of all to me. Sometimes, now, she straightened up from the hearth with a groan, rubbing her knuckles into the small of her back, for she was carrying a new child inside her.

Not many days later I pressed my cheek against Thunder's flank, stretching my arms around her swollen belly. There! Something inside thumped and shifted. Was it a little hoof dreaming of one day running over the ground? Thunder paid no attention but kept nosing through the long, dried winter grass, hunting tiny green shoots.

I pulled Thunder's head up to make her listen. "Soon your baby will come out. You must be a good mother and give it milk so that it will grow and run beside you. And you must teach it to be a horse that is a friend to people as you are. One day, perhaps, my people will have many horses that are the children of my good horse, Thunder."

I frowned then, thinking of my brothers. First Little Brother had woken that morning fussy and fretful, and then, for no good reason, Flint had lain back down on his sleeping robe and fallen back to sleep.

I had been hoping he would go with me to hunt birds' eggs and greens. Sometimes we felt hungriest in early spring, when there were starting to be new things to eat. It was a different kind of hunger than the gnawing ache of late winter, when the stored supplies were running out. Spring hunger was sharp and alive. We had to chase and climb and root in the mud for all the beginnings of a new season. One could almost feel warmth spreading out from the belly when it was finally full. I wanted suddenly to jump and dance and sing—or leap onto Thunder's back and tear madly over the ground into the torrent of mild air that was moving across the steppe from the south.

But I would not do that, because Thunder was a different creature now. She was a mare, heavy with a foal due to drop any day. She could run if she had to, but mostly she moved with a slow dipping, swaying motion, like a great chunk of ice floating high in a spring current. She had lost the foolish look of youth that liked to spook and bolt at every rustling leaf. Instead her eyes shone calm and wise, full of the mother spirit. She nudged me impatiently, as if to say that to her kind, and most especially to one of her kind in her condition, eating was more important than talking. I gave Thunder a final pat and picked up the bulging water skins I had laid down in the grass. My mother would be wanting them. I ducked through the doorway of our pit house.

Something was wrong. My father was making bundles of our bed robes, tying them up with rope. The first warm rains had not yet come. Surely it was too early to go to the fish camp? Grandmother held Little Brother in her lap, rocking him and trying to drip fever tea into his mouth from the corner of a soft piece of hide. Moss held Flint's head in her lap, helping him sip from a cup.

"Good—bring it here," my mother said, rising ponderously and moving to the fireside, dipping and swaying just like Thunder. She too would be birthing her baby very soon. I remembered the two babies born before Little Brother who had been laid, sweet and still, in the breast of the earth before they could reach their Naming Days. I thought of the ones before Flint and me whom I had never known. Even though Little Brother had almost reached his Naming Day, my parents looked to the coming of this new child with caution. They rarely spoke of it.

My mother's right hand strayed momentarily to her bulging middle. Then she seemed to catch herself and purposely take it away. I looked from one adult face to the other and saw fear. "What is it?"

Moss stooped, grunting softly, and pulled the hare-skin blanket away from Little Brother's naked chest. In the dim light from the fire and the open doorway, I could see that his flesh was covered with small, red spots. But it was his eyes that made my breath catch in my throat. They were huge, unseeing, and glazed like ice-covered stones in winter. In the corner Flint moaned and twisted sideways. Bark whined and licked my brother's face.

"It is the spotted fever," said my father. He sounded very tired. "It has not come to any of the other pit houses. We must leave the *b'ahut* and camp alone until it has passed. That is the way."

It was good that we had Thunder. She could carry the summer tent and sleeping robes as well as our cooking pots and what scant provisions we had this early in the season. I felt a little sorry to see her loaded so, with Flint sprawled among the many bundles that she dragged, but we were all burdened. Thunder walked steadily along, and my heart felt warm with pride in the strength of my horse. Moss carried a basket filled with her sewing tools and extra clothing. Old Flint held Little Brother in the crook of one arm. The speckled skin of Little Brother's naked thigh looked pale and smooth next to my father's weathered skin. There was a raised white scar from the tusk of a boar on Old Flint's forearm. His fingers were callused, the nails broken. The muscles of his biceps bulged. But he held Little Brother as softly and securely as my mother ever could.

"I can carry him," Moss said.

"No, you are burdened enough," he answered. His spear thrower was in his other hand, his pack on his back. Grandmother clutched her herb pouch on her hip and walked with a hand on my shoulder. A basket of household things thumped on my back. In my arms I carried a smaller basket. Inside it, within a clay pot, were coals from the fire. We had brought a bow and drill for fire starting, but bringing a few coals saved much labor.

The others of the *b'ahut* saw us off without coming close. There were a few quiet words and tense nods, but the fear was strong. No one else had the fever. It was best that we get away quickly. We crossed the river, Bark splashing happily beside us. There was a squawk, and Black left his perch to follow after us. He was not about to let his food supply get away.

We walked until sunset, north along the river to a knoll that rose out of the marshy grasslands. Here, where the biting insects would not be a torment, we put up our shelter. We dared not hobble Thunder with her foaling so near. Instead, my father and I devised a small enclosure for her with ropes in a grassy area between several scrubby trees. Silently I helped my father set up camp, make Grandmother, Moss, and the sick ones comfortable, and gather wood for the fire. Lastly I led Thunder down to the river's edge to drink.

Thunder dipped her muzzle into the water, and I watched the swallowing muscles ripple along her throat. The little spring frogs shrilled in the blue dusk. Thunder raised her head, letting trickles of water ring the pink surface of the stream. A long-legged fishing bird lifted out of the reeds on the far side and flapped downstream, blue-black against the rose-colored sky. I leaned an arm over Thunder's withers and a tear slid down my cheek. Silently my lips moved, singing the old Song to the Life Spirit:

At the dawn, at the noon,
In the dusk, in the dark,
For the new, for the old,
For the heat, for the cold,
Strike the spark,
Feed the coals,
Light the dark.

I could not remember the time when I had the spotted fever. Flint and I were very little, and for some reason he had not gotten it. I had lived. That was all I knew.

My fists clenched. I wished I could fight this thing as if it were some beast. I would not mind claws and teeth as much as this burning evil that could kill from inside. Then my face twisted, and for a few moments I allowed myself to cry. "Please let my brothers live," I sobbed into the empty air.

That first night Grandmother, Moss, and I sat up by turns drawing pebbles from the fire, dropping them sizzling into a pot to brew tea, crooning, humming, and rocking, always tending Flint and Little Brother. It was strange to try to hold up my twin brother, who had grown so much taller and stronger than me. He was like some big, helpless puppy. His head rolled on his shoulders like a little child who is sleeping deeply.

Old Flint slept or sat brooding at the entrance of the tent. Sometimes, when one of the sick ones groaned, I would see my father's big hands clench, his jaw tighten, and a haunted look cross his face. I looked at him, so powerful, this father who had always managed to protect us from prowling beasts. He had hunted and fed us in all the bitterest times that I could remember. I wanted to pound my fists against the muscles of his chest and cry,

"Make this sickness go away!" But he could not do it. For the first time, I realized that there were stronger things in this world than my father.

When I went out for water in the morning, I checked on my horse. The enclosure was empty! My stomach lurched. I looked around numbly, but Thunder was gone. Somehow she had worked her way under the ropes. I remembered how she had run back to the wild herd and stayed with them for much time. Life without my horse-friend had been so empty. Had she returned to the herd now to have her foal? Would she ever come back to me? I brushed away quick, hot tears. I must get the water. I could not think about Thunder now.

Sometime in the second night Flint began to talk, but it was not to us. It was dream talk, mumbling, then crying aloud, "Ahheee, Great One, for your teeth, claws, winter robe, flesh, I take your gift. . . ." I smiled to myself. Flint was talking to Bear Spirit. He had never killed one in waking life.

But Little Brother's lips were swollen and dry. He did not talk or dream anymore. In the gray time before sunrise, his body went limp and his spirit walked alone into the unknown world, away from our fire circle forever.

Grandmother began a high, thin wail of anguish. My twin brother slept the heavy sleep of exhaustion and did not yet know. Old Flint rose and walked slowly from the tent. Without looking back, my father walked away from the camp and out into the great empty grasslands. Bark whined but did not follow him. I tried to throw myself into Moss's arms, but my mother sat like a stone, no longer feeling or touching, not seeing or hearing.

Chapter Sixteen

Spring

For all that day and the next my mother lay, eyes wide, without moving. Grandmother and I finished the wailing, dug a resting place for Little Brother, lined it with what few early spring flowers and herbs we could find, and laid him in Earth Mother's body from where all life begins, with his face to Sun Father. And still Moss had not moved.

My father did not return to dig the hole or help with the burial. I did most of the digging myself, with the shoulder blade of a deer and a sharp stick. I felt no pain from the blisters and broken fingernails. I felt only anger. How could the Spirit of Life take Little Brother back when he was so close to his Naming Day? "I hate you, I hate you!" I sobbed over and over through clenched teeth, as I stabbed and dug at Earth Mother. How could my father just walk away now when we needed him most? I stabbed harder. Little Brother would have a proper grave, with or without my father.

We dressed him in his nearly finished Naming Day shirt. It had rows and rows of tiny river shells stitched to it, front and back. They gleamed like little moon faces and made a whispering sound as we put it on him. Grandmother placed a full bowl of dried meat and roots beside him though we had little to spare. We had left most of his toys behind when we went away from the *ahne,* but he was still never without Wolfie, so I tucked the tattered old wolf's tail under his arm. I found a small point in one of my father's tool pouches and lashed it with wet sinew to a green ash stick that I'd hardened in the fire. He would be sad without a toy spear. I dug a handful of clay from the riverbank and squeezed it into the shape of Thunder. A little of her spirit would be in the clay and could travel with him, perhaps even carry him, on his journey. There was no time to let the clay horse dry or harden it in the fire, and I could not bear it if it were to burst, as clay sometimes does. Besides, Little Brother loved to pinch and twist wet clay. I laid these things in his hands.

It does not make it any easier to bury him without a name, I thought. Why could not he have had a name? I knew I would never forget him, name or no name. Suddenly the thought came to me that three years or even three days could be a lifetime. Little Brother should have had a name, but now it was too late.

My brother Flint came and stood unsteadily beside us. He took off his precious wolverine tooth necklace and placed it around Little Brother's neck. Although he was a hunter now, and a man, silent tears rolled down his cheeks.

Just before we covered Little Brother, Grandmother tried once again to speak to Moss and make her come and see, but it was no use. Moss only lay on her side, staring into darkness. Grandmother and I crouched beside the grave, tucking Little Brother's sleeping robe around him. I watched old Touch-Sees run her gnarled fingers tenderly over her grandson's face to look at him one last time. I thought of my father walking coldly away and clenched my fists.

"Come," Grandmother said to Flint in a hoarse whisper, her voice nearly gone from wailing. "The women have prepared the dead. You must do the man's part." Flint's face was very pale, and his hands shook, but he pushed earth over Little Brother while Grandmother and I rocked on our heels and chanted the Song to the Spirit of Life.

On the fourth day, in utter silence, my mother labored and birthed yet again. I thought perhaps it was the child who birthed herself. She was strong and cried with hunger. Grandmother placed the babe on Moss's belly, but my mother turned her head away. The child found the breast and sucked, but no milk came. Grandmother screamed, "The Maker has given Life—you must feed it!" She slapped Moss's cheeks hard, but Moss only stared unflinching into the shadows.

The baby screamed with hunger. I put my hands to my ears. Flint watched silently from his bed. Grandmother clutched the child to her own gaunt frame and rocked and crooned until at last silence filled the tent.

A long time passed. I thought perhaps that Grandmother slept, but suddenly she spoke into the darkness. She spoke thoughtfully, as if remembering something from a time long gone. It was to me that she spoke. "The babe will die without milk. I have pain tea, and calming tea, and even milk tea, but the flower for sadness tea does not bloom until midsummer, and I have none left. Without it I cannot make your mother's milk come. Even with it I do not know. I have never seen grief like this." There was a long pause. Then: "You must take the baby to the river before your father returns. We will say it died during the birth—" Her voice broke. "It will be . . . faster that way."

It took a moment for me to understand what she meant. Then I shook my head even though Grandmother could not see me do so. "No, I cannot."

"You must."

"I will go back to the others. Maybe Rain or Weaver will nurse her."

"It is too soon. They cannot let you come back."

"I will try."

All that morning I ran back along the bank of the river with Bark trotting beside me, my infant sister held tightly in my arms. When the sun was high overhead, I stopped on the bank opposite the *b'ahut* and called to them. Slowly, they came to the water's edge.

"Please," I said, holding out my tiny sister in my two hands, "Little Brother has died. My mother is ill from sadness. It is as if her spirit died with him. She has no milk and will not try to nurse the new baby. Please take her. She is hungry." My sister whimpered.

Rain and Weaver, who both nursed babies of their own, looked at me brokenly across the water and shook their heads. "We cannot," Rain said, in a voice so low that I could barely hear it over the murmur of the river. "There has been fever at your fire. It is too soon. I am sorry." She put her hand to her mouth and turned away.

"At least give me sadness tea for my mother," I cried.

Weaver ran to her hut, came back, and tossed a small packet across to me. It landed in the water, but I quickly fished it out before it could become soaked through. I nodded my thanks, then started walking back toward my family's camp. I felt nothing. There was a bitter taste in my mouth. I was thirsty, but I could not bring myself to go so close to the river.

My sister stirred in my arms again and wailed, turning her cheek toward the touch of my arm. She was seeking milk. Was there any way of keeping her alive if my mother would not nurse her? She was growing weaker. I did not think she could live much longer. I looked at the river. It flowed deep and fast here. It was still high with spring runoff. I stared into the water. It was very green. I remembered the numbing chill of it when I'd waded across the morning that we left the *b'ahut*. Maybe Grandmother was right.

Suddenly my dog barked and rushed toward a willow thicket. I heard the sound of a large beast moving and tensed to run. Then I heard a familiar nicker. I walked forward, pushing the branches carefully aside. There was Thunder coming toward me. A stick-legged foal butted and stumbled beside her, trying to thrust its head under her flank.

Thunder stopped to pin her ears back at Bark, telling him to keep his distance. Afternoon sun flickered through the new willow leaves. Light and shadow glistened golden and brown on Thunder's sandy hide and the darker, fuzzy coat of her baby. I could see that it was another little mare, like her mother. The two of them seemed to glow with the Spirit of Life. Suddenly I knew what to do.

"Down," I said to Bark, and laid my little sister beside him in the grass. He nosed her carefully, looked at me, then laid his big head alongside her protectively.

I stepped toward Thunder slowly, ripping a piece from my shirt as I went. I had seen the fierceness of mares defending their babies, so I held out my hand to her, talking softly. Thunder came to me trustingly and thrust her muzzle into my hand.

"You have a baby," I said to her. "She is so beautiful, Thunder. See, I have a baby too. It is my sister. But Moss is sick with grief for Little Brother, and there is no milk. She has no heart to raise more babies."

Thunder's ears twitched at the sound of my voice.

She stood very still. The foal took her chance and drank thirstily, tail flicking all the while.

"Please, Thunder—" My voice broke. "Please can you give me some milk? She is a very little baby."

My hands moved along her sides now, stroking and loving my good horse. Thunder seemed to doze. Cautiously I found the other teat. I held the soft scrap of doeskin from my shirt cupped in one hand and tried to make the fingers of my other hand do what Thunder's baby was doing—sucking, pulling. Was there some magic to it? Nothing happened. I frowned and squeezed harder. Still nothing. Thunder turned to look at me. I wanted to cry with frustration. Then suddenly milk squirted hot into my hand. I tugged more gently, pulling the milk downward, and in a moment the bit of leather was soaked.

Hardly daring to breathe, I went to my sister and put a corner of the soft skin into her mouth. There was a pause. Then she sucked. In a few moments the skin was dry. She squalled for more. Four times I drew Thunder's milk from her and fed my tiny sister, until at last she was full and slept.

Then I plaited a makeshift rope of reeds and, holding my sister close in one arm, led Thunder and her foal back to the camp. I put the horses into the enclosure, hoping that Thunder would choose to stay there now. When I stepped into the tent, I saw that my father had returned to us. He looked up but did not meet my eyes, and I thought, *He truly looks like Old Flint now.* My heart suddenly twisted with pity for him.

They must have carried Moss to the river and bathed her, for now they were drying her and gently rubbing her skin with sweet herbs. She still stared, not knowing them. My twin brother sat by the fire sipping broth from a cup.

I laid the packet of tea in Grandmother's lap. Then I put my little sister into my father's arms. He touched his weathered cheek to the soft down of her head. A sound came from his throat like an animal in pain. Then tears flowed from his eyes. I had never seen my father cry before. I reached through the shadows for Grandmother's hand and placed it on the baby's full belly. My brother stretched out a finger. His new sister clutched it strongly and turned to stare at him with her dreamlike eyes.

I spoke to all of them. "This is my sister. My horse, Thunder, has given her life. I will care for her until my mother is well. She will live to see her Naming Day because today is her Naming Day. She is called Spring, and she is not going to die."

FOAL

At first this baby named Spring was content to suck milk from a soft piece of doeskin, but soon her appetite outgrew that. She choked if I tried to feed her from a cup. I did not know what to do until one day my father shot a deer with a fawn at her side. I looked at the doe's full little udder and thought sadly of her orphaned baby. Then suddenly I had an idea. With my father's help, I carefully skinned and cured the udder with the nipples attached. Then I cut off one nipple and sewed up the hole with the tiniest stitches I could manage. I filled it with Thunder's milk and tied the open end closed. My sister took to it right away.

I carried her on my back, sang to her, and kept her clean and fed. Grandmother and even my father and brother helped, but most of it I did myself. I was barely past my own childhood, but I had a love for our baby that was stronger, I think, than most older sisters feel, and the love seemed to grow out of caring for her.

She would waken each morning, soggy and sour faced, with a squall of emptiness. I tried always to have milk ready for her in her little leather pouch. Sometimes if the milk waited a time for her hunger, it would grow bubbly. Curious, I tasted it both fresh and bubbly, and both ways it was good. My baby sister thought so too. As she pulled the mare's milk into her body, she seemed to uncurl and bloom like a steppe rose, until satisfied, she turned, milky mouthed and bright-eyed, to greet the world.

For the first few days her eyes were the blue of a sky that brings rain, but soon they turned so brown they were almost black—a snapping, living black, like the wings of my crow. They were knowing eyes. I tried to make words for Grandmother to see their glowing wisdom. "Her eyes are like being outside and looking through the doorway of our pit house on a dark night and seeing the life within . . . or like staring into the fire, and seeing spirits dancing. . . ."

"Oh, I remember," Grandmother said in a reverent voice. "Each baby I have known had such eyes."

"But how can a baby know anything when she has lived only a few days?" I asked her.

"It is a mystery, Fern," she answered. "They are freshly come from the spirit world. I think perhaps they have come from somewhere very beautiful and *omu*."

"And Grandmother, just now when I spoke to her and looked into her eyes, I think she smiled at me—at least her mouth turned up and she had a look like sun on water. Why do babies smile?" I thought of my mother, like a husk of a person, almost as lost to us as Little Brother.

Grandmother was silent. Then she said, "You ask such big questions, Fern. Perhaps babies smile to help us look to light rather than darkness."

I stared at her. How was it that a woman growing close to the end of her winters, who could no longer see any light of this world, could look inside herself and see light? Then I turned my eyes toward my broken mother and wondered how a woman still strong of body, with years of life left to her, could be swallowed by darkness. And here, in my arms, was a creature who looked at this world of sorrow and joy for the first time and reached out her hands and chose joy.

Then Grandmother said something more. "Perhaps your eyes are a thing of wonder to Spring as well." She sighed. She and Spring could not share the eye magic. Then she reached out a twisted finger that was more like a dried root than something human and stroked the palm of my sister's hand until the tiny fingers closed around it. I saw in that moment that there is a whole world of skin touching skin; a way for two people to know each other without speaking or seeing.

The moon grew to *omu* again with no more fever before Old Flint and Grandmother said it was safe to go back. It was not yet time for the *b'ahut* to split apart for the summer, or we might have had to fend for ourselves until winter came again. We burned our tent, bedding, and clothing. Then we cleansed ourselves in the life water of the river, rubbed our bodies with sage, and put on new clothing that the others had made ready for us. It was nearly summer now, but the water was still cold. Little Spring screamed until her face turned red, but once she was dry, wrapped in a warm robe of hare fur given to her by Rain, with her belly full, she fell into a sweet-faced sleep. I think Rain would have taken her to nurse with her own baby, but Spring seemed to thrive on mare's milk, and by now I could not think of parting with her even if just until her weaning time. Without her

I think I too might have been swallowed up by the darkness of losing Little Brother.

Now that we had returned, the others, especially the women and girls, gathered around to admire our baby. Moss could walk now, but she did not speak and she seemed to need one of us to lead her by the hand. The other women shook their heads sadly when Moss did not return their greetings. Many of them knew the black-thought sickness, especially if a little one was lost, but it was not usual for someone to be so overcome by it.

I did not know if we should tell them that my baby sister lived on horse's milk, but when they saw me feed her, they soon learned for themselves why she had survived when my mother could not nurse her. The word spread like a fire in dry grass. Despite their suspicion of me, all the other women put their hands out to hold our baby. I could not help thinking that they just wanted a chance to look closely at her to see if she might be growing a mane and tail.

My brother Flint shivered as our father rubbed him dry after his bath in the river. He was still very thin. People did not say much about the fever. We try not to think about things like that once they are over. But Berry put her hand on my arm and whispered to me, "I am sorry for your Little Brother and for Flint." I looked at her and forgot all about the times that she had sided with Willow and the other girls against me. I loved my friend for her words.

I gave Thunder and her foal baths too, even though they did not like it very much. Already I could lead Thunder's baby, making her stop or turn the way I wanted. She followed me right into the river. Then she felt the coldness around her long legs, sniffed it, sneezed, and skittered like a spider! As I looked at her, I thought she might turn out to be yellow and black like her father, with the prettier shape of her mother. There was no white marking on her anywhere, but still I hoped she would have Thunder's kindness too.

"See?" said Flint to Cat Feet, taking the robe from around his own shoulders and rubbing the shivering foal with it. "Thunder's baby is already tame like her mother. Soon we will have another horse to carry us."

Suddenly there was something that I needed to do. Maybe it was a way of thanking the Spirit of Life for not taking my twin away from me. I knew it was not something I could take back once I had done it. I looked into Thunder's wise brown eyes. She looked steadily back at me. I stroked the colt's fuzzy coat that felt more like saiga fur than horse.

"Yes, you boasting brother of mine, when your little

horse has grown and you have taught her to carry you on her back, our people will have two horses to hunt with. We will never be hungry!"

"*My* horse?"

"Unless you do not want her," I said, looking at Flint sideways and trying not to laugh. "I could always give her to someone else—"

"Not *want* her?" Flint turned to me, so pleased that he stumbled and almost fell on his behind on the slippery riverbank.

I looked at my father. His eyes were warm. He nodded.

Then the others came forward with such skins and sleeping robes as they could spare for us until we could make more of our own. Any day, the *b'ahut* would be splitting up into the *ahnes* of summer, and we would need to construct a new tent. After we had made a fire and eaten, I went to check on Thunder and her foal. Flint was ahead of me. He had brought my horse comb. I smiled and helped him catch Thunder's baby. "Talk softly to her," I said in a low voice. "See how her ears turn as she listens to you. Then she does not think so much about the strangeness of the comb and try to get away."

Flint began gently to groom the little horse. "She is female, but still, her name is Hunter," my brother said. "I think she has grown since yesterday."

I put my arms around Hunter and smelled her sweet downy fur. "Long life of growing to you," I whispered. "My Naming Day gift for you is the gift of friendship."

Perhaps Hunter wanted a gift she could eat, for she reached out her little whiskered muzzle, closed her milk teeth over the end of the thong tying my hair back, and yanked it loose. I chased her all the way to the river before I got it back. What sort of a horse would she grow to be, sweet or wild? That was the beginning of wondering about Hunter.

Summer came. We packed our things and moved with the rest of our *ahne* to our first camp. Hunter scampered happily after us. Like any baby who is growing teeth, she seemed to think with her mouth. Every time I tried to brush Thunder or needed to crouch down to hobble her, a baby horse mouth would be all over me. It would start with nuzzling and chewing; then suddenly sharp little teeth would snap down on my earlobe, the back of my arm, even the place where I sit.

"Owww! Come get your little wolverine off me!" I would yell to Flint. Hunter nipped him as well. We did not like to spank her, but finally we had to, for the bites made purple bruises, and soon she might draw blood. Still, I did not think she did it for meanness.

"Even though they are mostly used for tearing grass, horses have powerful teeth," Old Flint warned us. "I have seen stallions with pieces of flesh hanging from their faces after a fight."

Often I would pick a bunch of tender grass as a treat for Thunder. Hunter was beginning to eat grass alongside her mother, and she quickly learned to eat these treats from my hand as well. One day when I had picked a small basket of blueberries and was walking home with them, I came upon a nice patch of onion roots. In the sling on my back, I could feel Little Spring stirring after a long nap. She would wake up hungry, so I hurried. I found a sharp stick and dug up a good bunch of the onions. Then, holding them carefully to the side so that the dirt would not get into my berries, I continued on my way. When they saw me, Thunder and Hunter came trotting forward. Thunder nosed the basket, turning away when I told her no, but before I could chase her baby away, Hunter helped herself to a mouthful of berries.

"No, you bad little horse!" I said, trying to swat her rump with the green ends of the onions. She reached for another mouthful and suddenly squealed in surprise. She pointed her muzzle at the sky, wrinkled her nose, and showed her pink gums and funny little stubby teeth. She had taken a great juicy bite from one of the onions!

"Aha, you thieving crow, how do you like the taste of *that* sweet?" I asked her, laughing. I offered her the onions again, but she backed up, blowing through her nostrils the way I used to do when I was little and played at being a horse. Then she threw her yellow rump in the air and scampered away.

My brother had trouble leading her in her rope bridle. She reared up and struck out with her front feet. Perhaps it was no different from the play of any other foal. In my heart I wondered if she had the strong, untamable nature of her father and all the other horses we had tried to ride. "She is just a baby—she will grow quiet and wise with time," my brother said. Yet I saw doubt in the lines between his eyebrows.

One morning after Spring was fed, Grandmother and I brought Moss down to the river to bathe. Flint had gone to dig cattail roots. My mother stared at her hands while I poured water over her and rubbed her skin with washing flower. It was good, sitting in the hot sun in nothing but our own skin. Spring lay on her blanket kicking her feet in the air. There was the cool, sweet smell of washing flower, and the watery breath of the river. I thought that if this were winter, we would freeze very quickly, sitting here on a rock with no furs to cover us. How strange that our world could change so much in just a few moon passages.

"Why does Sun Father let Earth Mother grow cold for so long each year?" I asked Grandmother.

"Perhaps to save us from being eaten to skeletons by gnats," she said, brushing the tiny insects away from Spring's face with the owl's wing fan that she always carried in bug season. She did not need to see them to brush them away, there were so many, despite the gnat-leaf we had rubbed on our skins. "Perhaps the snow is like a robe to keep Earth Mother warm while she grows all the baby things of the next year inside herself," she continued thoughtfully.

I closed my eyes, seeing winter, long and cold, yes, but also full of beauty. "Perhaps Sun Father gives us winter so that we can see tiny rainbow-colored sparks in the snow, and the steppe glittering white, turning to purple and pink as the sun goes down," I added.

Grandmother's face crinkled into a smile. "Perhaps he gives it to us so that we will truly appreciate a warm fire, a full belly, and a good story."

"Perhaps to make us strong, and full of courage . . . and hope," I said.

Grandmother felt for my hand and squeezed it. "Someday, I think, the name of the girl-who-tamed-the-horse will be spoken of around the fire. Keep hoping for your mother, Fern. The black-thought sickness is like a walking death, but it is a death that one can wake from in time. We will keep giving her sadness tea, and we will keep hoping."

Our new tent was very small. A fresh aurochs hide lay in the curing pit, waiting to be scraped, so we headed back to begin the task. As we drew close, we heard twigs cracking. Something big was moving slowly through the bushes. I felt my blood pound inside me. *Earth Mother, what was it?* It was nearly the size of a small bison, but I could not make out legs or a head. It seemed to lumber like a bear. I looked for black, shaggy fur. Then I saw that it had no hair at all. It was brownish and smooth, the color of cured hide.

Bark growled low in his throat, his shoulder fur bristling. I thought I might yell for my brother. Then the creature seemed to change shape, to run a few paces, before coming up against a scraggly bush and stopping. I tried to think of every beast I had ever heard of. What in all the world could it be? "Wait," I said to Grandmother. I was torn between wanting to run and wanting a better look at this unknown animal. I took a few steps closer, and now I could see lines upon the creature almost like stitched seams. Laughter bubbled up in my throat. They *were* stitched seams! This strange, misshapen creature stumbling through the bushes was our tent, with a foolish baby horse inside it!

"What is so funny?" asked Flint. He had come up behind us with his basket of cattail roots.

"That," I said, pointing to the tent-beast. "I think your little horse has been gobbled up by our shelter." Then I made a picture out of words for Grandmother. "Hunter is inside the tent, and it looks like a very fat woman, with no head, whose tunic keeps tripping her up. She keeps bumping into bushes."

Grandmother cackled soundlessly, her blind eyes squinting like crescent moons.

It took both my brother and me to free Hunter from the tangle of leather and rope and lead her back to Thunder again. She was frightened, but once she had filled her belly with her mother's milk, she did not look at all sorry. Instead, she lay down in the grass and rolled, then leaped to her feet again, shaking herself all over.

We spread out the tent to look at the damage. There were several long tears and a hole punched by a sharp little hoof. "I hope you like to sew," I said to Flint crossly.

It is strange that to have summer, we must have winter. To eat, we must kill and butcher. To carve a beautiful amulet, there must be blisters and finger pricks. There are so many opposites in the world. Often to have something nice, there must be something not so nice. So it is with hide curing.

We have several ways of doing it, depending on what sort of leather we want—fur on, fur off, soft and pliable, or hard as wood. Tent leather needs only to be scraped, to be buried in a pit of wet ashes for a few days, and then to have the hair stripped off. The smoke from our cooking fires finishes the curing. But to make leather for clothing, we take our bone-cracking hammer, split the skull of the animal to get at the brains, and rub the nasty, greasy, gray stuff into the hide.

The softest, whitest leather is made by soaking a hide in urine, and not even fresh urine. It is body water that has been saved until the smell of it burns the nostrils. We do this by tightly sewing up a hide so that it forms a container shaped almost like the animal itself. Little Brother had loved to be held up so that he could make his water right into this bag. The men do the same, and the women catch their urine in the wooden bowl we use at night to avoid going outside. As the hide fills and the smell grows more powerful, children dare each other to go up to it, sniff it, then run away, holding their noses and screaming.

Summer hides are not the best, but we were in need

of more clothing and several people had given us skins. Grandmother helped me sew the bag, and we hung it in a tree downwind of our camp. When it was nearly full of urine, I carefully stuffed in the hides, holding my breath against the stench, and pushing them down with a stick. Then I left it to stew for several days in the hot sun, like some sort of evil soup.

Two mornings later I awoke to hear my brother yelling, "No, Hunter!" I peered out of the tent. Thunder's foal was backed up against the tree, squeezing my tanning operation against the rough bark of the trunk as she scratched her rump. She nodded her head up and down, pleased to have found such a good, soft scratching post. Flint ran toward her with her bridle. The bag full of the soaking skins bulged dangerously.

"No!" I shrieked, but I was too late. There was a sudden noise like a snorting pig as it burst, and a waterfall of stale urine gushed all over my brother's little horse. In a panic she dashed to him for protection.

"Urghh! You creature from the refuse pits!" Flint cried, trying to push her away, but as he spoke, she lowered her head and shook herself, soaking him as well. Furious, Flint grabbed her chin, stuffed her head into her bridle, and dragged her to the river for a bath.

Grandmother and I were still laughing when he

returned. "At least my brother's hide will be soft, even if it does not smell sweet," I giggled, readying myself to run if he should try to hit me. But he ignored my taunt.

"I think I have discovered something," he said. "Watch this." He tugged on Hunter's bridle and led her away. Hunter began to scamper and half rear in her usual playful way, but Flint tugged at the loop of leather around her bottom jaw. I'd seen him do that many times. She usually ignored the tugs and kept on dancing as if she heard someone, somewhere, playing a bone flute that we could not hear. But this time she quieted and looked at him with eyes that seemed to say, "I will listen to you now."

"How did you do that?" I asked.

"When I put her bridle on to take her to the river, I was so angry, I hardly knew what I did. Somehow, I got the loop *over* her tongue instead of *under* it. It seems to make her listen. Maybe that is what she needs."

Later Flint fixed a smooth piece of bone to her bridle so that it rested across her tongue. This worked even better than the rope. She would always have some of her father's spirit, but my brother had discovered the tool for managing her. It was a tool we would come to use on other horses.

Chapter Eighteen

FEAR

It was a good summer and sped by quickly, with our two babies, horse and human, growing almost as quickly as the grasses on the steppe. Perhaps it was the healthy, sunny smile of Little Spring, or the sight of me milking Thunder for her food, or the funny, friendly, irresistible nature of Thunder's foal, but people seemed to have forgotten to shun me. There were those in the *ahne* who still eyed me with suspicion, but most people saw how useful my horse was. Thunder allowed others to ride her or use her to work for them, so perhaps I was not a witch or a magician after all.

Because of the baby I tended, there was a difference

in the way the other women treated me, almost as if I were one of them. They were generous with advice, outgrown clothing, and stories about their own children.

I was now fourteen winters old. Several girls younger than me were already married. As fall and the Feast of *Omu* approached, I began to think about young men. My blood cycle came and went with each moon, and I felt ripe with the secret knowledge that now I was a woman. I had told no one. Yet one day Grandmother took my hand as I came up from the river and said, "Why have you not told us that you are a woman?"

"How did you know?" I stammered.

She cackled. "When a girl is cranky one moment and sings like a lark the next, and does much washing of her things, an old grandmother guesses!"

I gripped her hand. "Please, you must not tell," I begged.

"Is it because of Badger?"

"I would rather die than marry him."

Too soon the time came when the *ahnes* straggled back to the *b'ahut* for the winter. Young men came to talk to me about Thunder—or perhaps just to talk to me, I was not sure. I taught them to ride her and to hunt from her back, as long as they treated her kindly. Sometimes now

I wished my hair did not still hang long over my back like a girl's.

Wing and Cat Feet had become hunters, but I had known them since we ran about bare bottomed together. I could not forget how Wing once threw up his meal upon the ground and partly upon me when we were spinning like snow devils to see who would fall down first. I could hardly look at Cat Feet without seeing his finger in his nose the way it always used to be when he thought no one was looking. They were too much like brothers to interest me.

Still, there were other young men whom I watched slyly, trying not to let my eyes catch theirs, for if they did, my face grew so hot that I knew they could see the redness of my cheeks. Falcon had a face that was beautiful to look at, and he laughed easily. Runner had a puppy that I was sure Bark had fathered. I liked the way he spoke to and played with it.

Secretly, from a safe distance, I watched Badger. He was very strong, and in some lights he could be almost good-looking. I noticed that he did seem to have a way of never returning from a hunt without game. I almost thought that if he could be taught to clean himself, he might not be so ugly.

But Bark would not stop growling if Badger came

near me, and the one time I allowed Badger to ride my horse, he kicked her and yanked at her bridle until tears came to my eyes. When he was finished, she was wild-eyed and lathered, and there were raw places at the corners of her mouth. I was shaking with rage as he finally leaped off and threw her reins to me. I walked far over the steppe with her until she was calm again and the sweat had dried on her body. But I was not calm. My rage had hardened into a lump in my chest so tight that it hurt. Why had I been so foolish? Never would I let him touch my horse again.

One morning, as I was gathering greens near the east *kolki*, my sister asleep in a sling on my back, I heard angry voices. I walked closer until I could see who it was. Flint and Wing were standing beside the carcass of a young sow. Badger crouched beside it, holding up a dart.

"I will not hunt with one who speaks untruth," said my brother. "I saw Wing's dart as it struck."

"You can say what you like," said Badger with a smile, as he pulled the dart from the sow's neck, "but this is *my* dart. Wing's dart lies over there."

Wing walked over and picked up his dart, looking closely at the point. "I see no blood, but if it had struck the ground, I would see dirt on it."

"Look, there is a patch of blood on his leggings

where he rubbed your point clean," said Flint to Wing. "And the wound is torn where one dart was yanked out and another thrust in. That is what we get for letting Badger run forward first."

Badger sprang to his feet and grabbed my brother by the throat of his shirt. "It is *my* kill!" he snarled.

"I have several more darts," said Wing quietly. Badger looked up to see that Wing's dart was now aimed at him. He let Flint go.

Flint loosened his shirt from his neck and brushed at it as if there were filth on it. "Let Badger have the *honor* of the kill, and also the honor of carrying it home," he said in disgust.

I kept my eyes down as Badger passed me, grunting under the weight of the sow. Now I knew how it was that he seldom returned from a hunt without game. The meat would be shared, regardless of who killed it, but the honor would be his. I could never love a man who would steal honor.

It was several months before Badger learned I had given Thunder's foal to my brother. When he did, he was very angry. In the early part of winter, much time was spent hunting while the game was still fat from summer, but once the cold was truly upon us, Flint spent time every day leading Hunter with the small bridle he had made for her. Thunder's daughter was still full of baby-horse foolishness, but she would follow, with little scampers and bucks, when Flint led her along. It was the day that Flint first fastened a strap around Hunter's middle that Badger said to Cat Feet, "He acts as if he owned her," and Cat Feet answered, "Did you not know that Fern gave her to him?"

Later, as I crouched beside Thunder, milking her for my sister's food, there were sudden footsteps in the snow behind me. I rose, turning swiftly. Badger loomed over me. My brother had led Hunter away once Thunder had let down her milk so that I could get a share for our sister more easily. For once Bark had followed Flint instead of me, and I was alone. Fear rose in my chest until I could barely breathe.

"You had no right to give the foal to Flint," he said. "By rights it is mine, as you will soon belong to me."

"I will never belong to you!" I do not know how I had the courage to say that, for I was sure he would strike me then.

He did not hit me, but he gripped my arm, making blue marks that did not go away for many days. His face was black with anger. "I will kill any other man who tries to have you." His eyes narrowed to slits. "I think I will not wait until you are a woman. I have waited long enough. The horses should be mine, for my father grows old, and soon I will be the strongest hunter."

He said no more but stalked away.

That night he spoke again to my father in the doorway of the pit house, while I hid, sick with terror, in my sleeping robe. My mother sat by the hearth, not seeming to know what was happening.

She could sit up now, but she still did not speak or meet eyes with us, and if we put Spring into her arms, there was no strength or will in them to hold her. The rest of us fed Moss from a spoon, making her swallow enough to stay alive. Grandmother and I brewed cup after cup of sadness tea and made her drink it like a little child. We all took turns feeding, rocking, and tending her baby. I thought my brother Flint must be the only young hunter in the entire *b'ahut* who was willing to change the wrappings of an infant, but ever since he had pushed the earth over Little Brother's grave, he had changed. He fetched wood and water when he saw they were needed, with no complaint, and he as well as my father saw when Grandmother and I grew weary caring for Moss and the baby. There was no talk of men's or women's work. If warm water was needed, it was fetched. If Spring cried with a belly pain, one of us took her and walked back and forth with her until she eased and slept.

Now I was almost glad Moss had not yet come out from inside herself. I heard the harsh sound of Badger's voice and the quiet tone of my father as he answered, but not the words. When at last Badger had gone, my father came in to me. I sat up in my bed, dreading what he might say.

"I am sorry, Daughter," he began.

I felt myself grow cold.

Then he continued, "Badger is a strong and skilled young hunter. Marriage to him would bring much honor . . ."

There was a rushing sound in my ears.

Then finally I heard the smile in his voice. ". . . but I cannot allow him to marry you. It is the horses he wants. He has no particular regard for you. I do not like him, or his ways—"

I leaped up and threw my arms around my father's neck. "You are the wisest and best father!" I cried. "How can I ever thank you?"

Over in the corner Grandmother was hugging herself and cackling. She had kept quiet this whole time. Now she said, "Well, I guess I do not have to feed nightshade tea to that puffed-up young bull after all."

"You are an evil old woman," my father told her, but there was laughter in his voice. He shook his head and smiled at me. "I think she really might have done it." Then he grew serious again. "Do not thank me," he said gently. "I would not have my beautiful daughter sad or unloved. But we must take care. I do not trust him, and as I said, he wants the horses."

Chapter Nineteen

Bark

Moss's spirit came back into her body on one of that winter's coldest days, when Spring was nearly ten moons old. For some time now my little sister had been crawling about and pulling herself to a standing position against the sleeping benches. This pleased her mightily. She would pat her hands against the furs, crinkle up her face into a grin, and squeal until somebody looked at her. But on this day, there was no one to look at her except the silent woman who sat in the corner staring into the fire.

I was out checking snares. I rode Thunder, with Hunter tagging along, chewing at my leggings and making a nuisance of herself. Flint and our father were away on a long hunt with the other men. They had left Thunder home so that she could tend to her foal, although Hunter was big and husky and almost completely a grass eater now. This was her first winter, and no one wanted to take any chance of losing our second tame horse.

Grandmother had heard Singer's voice calling through the doorway, "Grandmother Touch-Sees, Lark has got the barking cough. Can you brew a tea for her?" Spring was napping like a tired puppy among my sleeping robes, and Grandmother did not want her to catch any sickness, so she asked Singer to send Painted Sky to watch the baby while she went to brew the tea. But Painted Sky had stopped on the way to talk to Willow.

Meanwhile Spring must have woken up. When she realized that there was no one home who would laugh with her and tell her what a big girl she was for sliding out of bed and standing up, she began to cry. Maybe she pulled herself around to where the silent woman was sitting and patted and tugged at her face, trying to make her look at her. Maybe then she pulled the bone hairpin from Moss's bun and buried her little fat fists in the river of graying hair that tumbled down. Maybe when Moss still did not respond, she cried for me or Grandmother and worked herself over to the doorway where she saw us come in and go out. Somehow she pushed against the heavy skins and, despite the stinging air, crawled outside. It is easier to push our door covering outward from inside than to lift it to get back in, especially for a tiny child.

Sound does not carry well through the walls of pit houses, and no one was outside to see her. If she had remained in the cold very long, she would have died, for she wore only a shirt that she had nearly outgrown.

But Bark had run ahead of Thunder and me on our way home. When I left the horses and came to our dooryard, I heard Spring squalling and saw my mother sitting in the snow, weeping, with her face buried in Bark's fur. Moss had not come outside by herself since Little Brother died. I ran to her and saw that she held my baby sister tightly in her arms.

"The dog, Bark, woke me," Moss said over and over. "This baby was out here crying, and he came inside and woke me."

It was too late for Moss to be able to make milk for my baby sister, but it did not matter, for Spring was growing teeth and beginning to eat soft food, and besides, Thunder still had plenty of milk for her. It was strange to see Moss holding Spring and talking softly to her, a look of wonder on her face. My heart said she was *my* baby as well as my sister, but I knew that it was good that the Spirit had given Spring back her real mother. Grandmother cried more tears than one could ever imagine might pour out of her little dried-up body, mumbling thanks to the Spirit of Life over and over for the return of her son's wife.

The next day my father and brother came home with shares of meat for our family. When Old Flint came through the doorway, Moss was holding Spring in her lap, singing. She looked up at my father and smiled. His face crumpled. He went to her and knelt by her side, weeping, and she held him as if he were another of her children.

When he lifted his head again, he noticed Bark curled up on the floor beside my sleeping bench. "Why is the dog in here?" he asked, laughing now.

"The dog, Bark, is Spirit Uncle to our children. He may sleep where he pleases," my mother answered.

My mother's hair was grayer and she had lost both flesh and strength. She did not recover all at once, but she tried to do her part, one small task at a time.

I did not know what I felt for this mother person who had not accepted my friendship with horses and animals, who had turned away from me, then broken down completely at Little Brother's death. I was angry with her when she could not or would not feed my baby sister. I was angry when, in her pain, she could not be a mother to me. Every other girl my age had been given a Woman's Feast. Any other mother would have guessed when her daughter's blood cycles started.

Then, for a long time, I knew only pity for her. And now I knew that I did not really need her anymore in the old way that a girl needs her mother. I, who could tend a baby, could certainly take care of myself. Yet even though she could not at first do a woman's full share of work, everything seemed easier now that she was back with us.

At first Moss said very little, but soon she began to ask questions. The first question came as she watched Spring drinking Thunder's warm milk from a cup, which she was able to do now.

"What are you feeding her?"

Her eyes grew wide when I told her.

"Would no one nurse her for you when I could not?"

"It was too soon after the fever to return."

She closed her eyes with the pain of knowing what would have happened without Thunder's milk. Little by little we told her how our baby had survived, how long it had taken Flint to get his strength back, how long she herself had been ill. Very gently Grandmother and I told her about how we had buried Little Brother, and about how Old Flint, too, had broken down at that time.

"I am so sorry," she said.

I put my hand on her arm. "You could not help it," I whispered. "And now you are strong again." As I said those things to her, I felt a heaviness lift from my spirit. I remembered that this was the mother who had not allowed me to die when I was born an extra baby. She had loved each of her children fiercely. Perhaps losing some of them had made her hold on harder to me and in that holding she had pushed me away. How was it that forgiving my mother helped to heal my own heart?

Moss quickly fell in love with Little Spring, as anyone would have. No baby ever had a more winning smile or such wise, shining eyes. Often now I saw Moss watching Thunder grazing contentedly with her foal at her side. She saw how I milked the mare, and how Flint and I taught little Hunter to carry a small load on her back.

In early spring Moss busied herself gathering tufts of shed fur. I thought she was making a rug, but I had never seen her work felt with such care. She decorated it with designs of blue and white flowers and sewed rows of river shells along the edges. What sort of rug was this to be? It was too beautiful for dirty feet to step upon.

Then one morning, as I was tending my horse, my mother walked out to us with the rug in her hands. She said, "I have noticed that when the horse runs hard, she sometimes sweats much. This will keep your seat and legs dry."

I could barely speak. "It is so beautiful. Thunder and I thank you."

Hesitantly she slipped the rug over my horse's back. "And I thank your horse, Thunder, for saving the life of my child when I was too weak in my heart to care for her. I owe you thanks, as well, Fern, for tending your sister—and me—all this time. I know it was not easy for you." This last she said in a whisper, staring at the ground.

"I am a woman now," I said to her.

"So much time—I should have known." She closed her eyes for a moment. Then she opened them and smiled. "Yes."

Then my mother looked hesitantly at me and asked, "Will you teach me this thing of getting milk from your horse-friend so that I can at least help to feed our baby, Spring?"

Our baby? How my heart thanked her for saying

that! I did not throw my arms around her then, though a part of me wished to. Instead I took her hands and, squatting by her side like friends, I showed her how to gently pull milk from Thunder's teats.

Chapter Twenty

Flight

"There must be someone," said Berry. She was helping me gather the buds of the washing flower. Moss and Grandmother were giving me my Woman's Feast at last.

"No, really," I said. "There are some I like, but nobody special. I am just glad that my father has said no to Badger."

Berry turned and looked at me then. "It is good that the *ahnes* will split up for the summer soon. You must still be careful of him."

I nodded. Then a smell of roasting hazelnuts and honey came to us. We looked at each other and grinned.

"Your brother will be drooling!"

"Let him drool—this is my feast! The men must cook for themselves tonight!"

The tent for my Woman's Feast was raised when we came up from the river. Each woman brings a piece from her own summer tent, and the pieces are all laced together to make one. A group of little girls watched enviously when we entered. My heart thumped as I stooped and came through the doorway. All the women of the *b'ahut* were seated in a circle around my mother and grandmother, who sat beside the fire in the center and held out their hands to me. I looked at all the smiling faces of old, young, and middle-aged women. I saw the love and wisdom of mothers, sisters, aunts, and friends in their good faces. The one tent, which they had made together, sheltered us. I could scarcely believe that all this was for me.

My mother poured warm water over my head, while Grandmother made a paste of the flower buds. Then together they washed my hair, and rinsed and combed it out while it dried in the warmth of the fire. It shone softly in the firelight, rippling over my shoulders and arms. I lifted a strand to my face. It smelled sweetly of the washing flower.

At last Moss gathered my hair into a bun at the nape of my neck. Then Grandmother put an ivory hairpin into my hands. It was yellow with age and smooth from much use. The end of it was carved into the shape of a horse's head. I gasped.

"You are not the first woman of our people to love horses," she said to me. "My mother, whose name was Wind, never touched a living horse, but she, too, loved to watch the children of Hekwos run. She would want you to have this." There was a murmer of satisfaction from the women around us.

My hands were shaking too much to put the hairpin in by myself. As Moss slid it into place, she said, "When I see the strong and beautiful woman you have become, I thank Earth Mother and Sun Father for your life, for giving me the courage and strength to raise both my twins. I was wrong ever to doubt that choice."

We feasted then on tender meats, a rich soup, and sweet nut cakes. Weaver poured a dark liquid from a skin bag into a small cup and held it out to me. I put it to my lips and for the first time tasted fermented berry juice. When I wrinkled my nose, all the women laughed. They gave me gifts then, not things, but words that would come back to me later, when I needed them most: *You are stronger than you know. Honor the friendship of women. Seek joy. Laugh . . .* We all laughed much and even cried a little. Finally the stepping-out time came.

All the other women went out of the tent first. I suppose it was to make sure the young men would know to look when at last I appeared.

It was true. All eyes were on me—my father's glowing with pride, my brother's also warm but a little bit laughing. The little girls had gathered again to watch. Painted Sky tugged shyly at my skirt and whispered, "You are beautiful, Fern." I smiled at her.

My cheeks burned. The nape of my neck felt bare and exposed. I had been a woman secretly for many months, but a voice inside me sang joyfully, *Now I truly am a woman!* Cautiously I glanced around. There were Cat Feet and Wing and several other young men watching. I kept my eyes down and tried not to smile. Everyone would go to their own pit houses now. It was almost over. Then I saw him. Our eyes met for an instant before I looked at the ground again. But that was enough. Badger was standing, arms folded, watching me through slitted eyes. As I watched, he deliberately spat on the ground. A shiver ran down my spine.

I found that Badger often watched me after that, but whenever I noticed his eyes on me and my horse, I would turn my head and see that my father was busy nearby. Perhaps he would be slicing thin strips of venison for my mother to hang on the smoking racks. Or if not my father, I would see my brother outside the pit house, tending a small fire for heating boiled birch sap and fletching darts. My father and brother had always hunted together since the day that Flint became a hunter and a man, but now only one at a time went with the others. I did not fear Badger so much because I knew that my father and brother would protect me.

To thank them, I decided Thunder and I should travel across the river, a day's ride away, to where we seek our good gray flint. It was a beautiful spot, this place where the sister of our river cut through a bank of gravel before winding westward. Here we found flint nodules bigger than a man's fist. Thunder could carry as much flint as several men, and my father knew that I had an eye for selecting choice material.

The ice breakup was over. There were blushes of silver pink in the willow buds and a tinge of palest green where Sun Father had begun to waken the grassland. A lark was singing high up in the great blue air-world above the earth-world. What did Thunder and I look like to him? Were the two of us a tiny spider-animal crawling across the hugeness of the steppe?

We were thirsty by the time we got to the river. I had brought a throwing stick and darts in case I saw game or encountered some beast. I slid to the ground, unslung them from my shoulder, and crouched by the water's edge.

We were drinking, Thunder reaching down with her long neck, Bark lapping with his great tongue, and me flat on my belly, scooping water up in my hands, when I heard a voice behind me.

"I will take the horse."

It was Badger!

"There is a herd of her kind near the east *kolki*, and I would taste horse meat tonight."

Before he could move a step closer, I leaped to my feet and up onto Thunder's back. "Bear spoke for me when I tamed her," I cried. "He said that no one will ride her without my word, and I say *no*!"

He grabbed her bridle and held it. Thunder snorted nervously, feet dancing on the slippery river cobbles. Bark crouched close by, growling. "Bear is not here. With or without you as my mate, the horse will be mine."

"You will have to kill me before I would give myself or my horse to you."

He smiled. "Then perhaps I should do that."

I could not believe what he had said. "My father and brother would kill you also," I screamed in a shaking voice. "Let go of my horse!" I jerked at the reins and kicked

Thunder so that she moved sideways, half dragging Badger into the river up to his knees. He was ready with his axe for Bark, who sprang then, lips drawn back in a raging snarl. As my dog leaped toward him, Badger swung the side of it into Bark's skull just above his eye, sending him flying back against the gravel bank. He did not get up.

Badger laughed and stepped close now, a huge fist on each of Thunder's reins. "If you should fall from your horse and strike your head on a rock, there would be much wailing over your body, but there would be no one to blame. Once I have the horse, there are those who would follow me. An axe and a rock leave the same mark." He reached for my arm to drag me from my horse's back. That is when I spat into his eyes and again kicked Thunder's sides.

She hardly needed it. She galloped over him, dragging him underneath her along the streambed until her bridle broke away. Cursing, he fell onto the rocks. Using my legs, I guided her, splashing up to her belly, across the river. It was as she was scrambling out on the opposite bank that I felt Badger's dart strike my shoulder. I thought he had hit me with a rock until I felt the shaft bouncing against Thunder's rump. The impact knocked me sideways and nearly off, but somehow I clung to her neck.

I do not know how far or in what direction Thunder galloped. I only held on, with a blackness growing before my eyes. The dart must have shattered when I finally did fall to the ground. I do not know how long I lay there.

I awoke to a whimpering Bark beside me. One side of his head was a bloody, swollen mess that made me want to retch, but he was alive. My eyes wandered without my body moving. Thunder cropped grass a few steps away. I was on my side. After a time my eyes strayed to the throbbing of my shoulder, and I saw the point of Badger's dart protruding through my shirt just under my collar bone. I coughed and put a hand to my mouth. There was no blood, so I knew that my lung had not been pierced.

I was told later that it was good I did not have the strength to pull the dart out or I might have bled to death. I tried to haul myself to my feet with Bark's help, but I could not do it. I rested. After another time I whistled, with what small breath I had, to Thunder. She lifted her head, then walked to me and nosed my face as if asking why I did not get up. I used her leg to drag myself upright. I could not climb onto her back. It was all I could do to stay on my feet, hang on to her mane with my good left arm, and put one foot in front of the other.

I knew no direction; I knew only that I must move and that I must try to stay with Thunder. With her I would be easier to spot if my father or brother came looking. My poor dog stumbled beside me, his head cocked to one side like an old dog that has had a fit and is about to die.

I did not know then why Badger did not track me. If it were discovered what he had done to me in his rage, he would be severely punished. He should have been trying to make sure I was dead so that he could hide my body, for there was no way that anyone could make a dart in the back look like an accident. The flesh between my shoulder blades crawls now as I tell this, thinking that he might have been following me, but my brain could not think very clearly then. The pain in my shoulder was like a white light that burned everything before it. . . .

Harsh laughter . . . the butt of a javelin poking my leg . . . I did not know that I had fallen, but I was on the ground again. It was not Badger. Several voices were speaking a language I did not understand. I opened my eyes to see five men, a hunting party, standing and squatting around me. Their bodies were lean and long limbed, as if made for running. Their faces were tattooed, making their teeth and the whites of their eyes stand out against black swirls, zigzags of skyfire, lines of dots. I cowered away from them. Bark struggled to his feet, growling, and they laughed again. They were Night People.

One of them bent and lifted the hair from my face. He spoke more strange words in a mocking tone, and the others laughed yet again. I thought I heard a word like our word for *bird*, and I realized that it was not the words that were so different but the way they came from deep in the man's throat, almost as if he were growling. He clucked his tongue, touching the spear point in my shoulder, then spoke some more words, something that sounded like *gift* and *brother*. The others roared with laughter, nodding vigorously.

Then I saw that one of them, with broken, yellow stumps of teeth and patterns like snakes across his cheeks, wore Badger's axe tucked into the belt of woven hemp about his waist. A taller man, wearing a wolf-skin shirt, held Badger's darts and throwing stick. I recognized the white goose fletching and the crudely carved animal that was meant to be a badger on the end of the spear thrower. Badger was no artist, but I had seen it many times. I was not sorry if Badger was dead, but these Night men were not any less terrible.

They looked at Thunder grazing nearby, and as I

watched, one with a heavy lower jaw like a boar's gestured and lifted his weapon as if he would kill her. Two others set their darts, but the fourth grabbed the first man's arm and pointed as Thunder swung her head around and the white marking on her hindquarter could clearly be seen. They gazed at each other with round eyes and began speaking in whispers.

I forced myself into a sitting position and whistled the eagle's call to Thunder. Her head came up and she trotted to me, unafraid of the men. The men backed away, speaking in hushed tones. They glanced with fear and wonder from Thunder to me. Once more I clawed my way to a standing position with the help of my horse. The men did not help. I tried to tell them that if they would lift me up, she could carry me, but that was an idea that they could not comprehend.

Instead, one of the men, who was built with the same sinewy strength as a cat, picked me up and slung me over his shoulder. I do not know how long they walked. Dimly I was aware that it began to rain heavily. I hung in a swaying twilight world with only the steady jarring of each step keeping me from sliding into a place of nothingness. I do not know if they led Thunder or she simply followed after me with Bark.

We stopped finally, and there were other voices,

some asking questions, some laughing. The rain still poured down. The boar-jaw man bellowed something in a jeering tone, and the cat man who carried me stooped through the doorway of a pit house and dumped me onto a sleeping bench. He spoke to someone, but there was no answer. Bark licked my hand where it dangled over the side of the bench. How had he been allowed inside? A brand from the fire was held close, but the face behind it was hidden in shadow. A knife cut the shirt way from my shoulder, and there was an indrawn breath, but still no words.

Then I heard a girl's voice speaking the strange language, but sounding a little more like my tongue. She asked something about water. Hands turned me onto my side, others held my head firmly. A piece of hide was forced between my teeth. Then a hand like stone gripped my injured shoulder and another took hold of the dart point and pulled.

Chapter Twenty-One

WORTHLESS

Daylight . . . so hot . . . *please* . . . water . . . thrashing . . . freezing . . . soaking wet . . . sweat . . . freezing again . . . darkness . . . *please, I am so hot . . . Earth Mother, do not take me* . . . daylight . . . whimpering . . . *Bark? Thunder?* . . . darkness . . . I am floating in the river . . . the sky is white . . . no pain . . . Sun Father . . . golden light . . . warm . . . hare eyes . . . *Little Brother!* . . . he smiles, shakes his head . . . *Go back, Fahnie* . . . daylight . . .

When I opened my eyes, it was to my fourth life, for three times now I had looked death in the face and still lived. Once it had been simply attacking beasts, then the beast of winter, and lastly a beast that was a man. I stared up at the underside of a reed-and-mud roof laid over saplings, just like my own home, but I knew by the smell that I was in a strange place. It was not a stink of filth, but a dense, complicated smell of many herbs—spicy, bitter, rank—some I knew, some I didn't. Bunches of dried leaves and roots hung from the ceiling. I smelled a dog smell too, not such a good one.

"Bark?" A tongue licked my hand. "You live!" My voice was a whisper. I tried to move so that I could see him, but it was as if my body lay under a great weight. I closed my eyes.

It seemed only a moment, but when I opened them again, it was dark once more. A fire burned brightly, and beside it a burly figure squatted, half sitting on one leg, doing something. Washing something. A dog. Bathing the face and the shoulder of a dog.

"Bark?"

My dog did not race to me like the spirit of joy, wagging, licking, woofing, as he used to do when we had been parted. He got to his feet stiffly, slowly, his head still cocked to one side almost as if he were drunken. But he came. I could tell from the sound of his whimpering that inside him his heart was full of joy. He laid his big head on the bench beside me, and I was able to move my good hand enough to touch him. The side of his head was still one great, draining wound. I could see that the bone above his eye had been crushed. The eye was gone. How could it be that he lived? Tears poured out of my eyes for my dog.

The person by the fire rose and moved awkwardly toward me. He limped like an old man, but his body was muscled like that of a young man. A Night man. I felt a surge of terror. What use that Badger had not killed me? I had been captured by the Night People. Was not that equally fearful?

I could see his face now. He did not look much older than me, perhaps sixteen or seventeen winters, but it was a face that could not be read. He did not have the fearful tattoos of the others. His eyes stared at me but told me nothing. He said nothing. He touched my forehead briefly with the back of his hand, nodded, hitched his way back to the fire, and returned with a cup. Without seeing if I could lift my head, he slid a hand under it and put the cup to my lips.

"Uhhhhhhhh!" Pain so that for a moment I could not see.

He waited, then put the cup to my lips again. I swallowed once. So bitter. After that he gave me water and I swallowed some of it gratefully, for my mouth felt as dry and cracked as the earth in summer. Then I was overcome with a huge tiredness, as if I had walked for a year of days. I slept.

It was a long while before I could sit up and eat from a bowl by myself using my left hand. My right arm could feel, but it would not work. The limping person who did not speak had bound it to my side so that my shoulder should not move. I lay mostly on my left side to allow the wound to drain both ways. Each time I woke, I sniffed, expecting to smell the sickening odor when such a wound begins to poison the body—the smell that comes before death. But now that the fever was passed, the wound remained clean.

Bark stayed beside me. I watched as the silent person tended my dog's wound as well. He did not seem to know what it was to have a dog for a friend. At first he was cautious, pushing small pieces of meat toward Bark's muzzle and snatching his hand away as if this poor, sick animal that could barely move would bite him.

My dog could not eat by himself, so the silent one tried to spoon broth into his mouth. Bark moved his tongue and swallowed a little, but most of the broth ran out onto the floor. Finally the Night man had to lift up his head and hold it in his lap. When Bark could swallow no more, the man continued to sit that way for a while. Cautiously he ran his hand over my dog's fur, and I knew that he was enjoying the softness and warmth of the fur of a living animal.

When he took his hand away, Bark thumped his tail weakly on the floor. The silent one stared. He stroked Bark's shoulder again and watched the tail. Again it thumped. Then Bark licked his hand.

Bark did not fear this Night man, so my fear lessened somewhat. The man must be a healer, I thought. Sometimes he went out and did not come back for a while. I watched while he prepared himself. He wore long breeches even now with the weather warmer. The first time he pulled up his leg covering and I saw that he had no foot, my stomach lurched. I had never seen such a thing. His leg simply ended where his anklebones should have been. He had a carved piece of wood, thin and hollowed to the shape of his calf at one end, and heavy at the bottom, which he lashed to his leg with thongs, in place of the foot. In the pit house he took it off, for the thongs left deep grooves and calluses in his flesh. But when he went out, he lashed it on and, leaning on a stick, was able to walk after a fashion.

My pain was duller now, unless I moved too quickly, but it was a thing, like a shadow, that did not go away.

Sometimes it made me so tired that I could only sleep. Other times it would not let me sleep, and I could do nothing but stare into the shadows, listening to the rain that continued endlessly, waiting for time to pass. This much rain would make the rivers too high to cross. When the water went down again, all tracks would have been washed away. The world is a very big place, and I had no idea where in it I was. How would my father and brother ever find me?

Now and then an older woman came and tended me. Her hair was thin and gray, and she had haunted eyes. But her fingers were gentle. They washed the hole that was in me, changed the packing of drawing herbs, or gave me a drink that made my brain fuzzy so I could rest. She did not speak much to me, but when she did, her words had a gentleness that made me yearn for Moss and Grandmother Touch-Sees. Her word for *child* was the same as ours. When she said it and touched the curve of my cheek, tears sprang to my eyes. I noticed that often when she got to her feet, she groaned softly, holding her belly, and I thought she must be ill. She spoke quietly to the silent man. Still no words came from his mouth, as if he lived in his own place, outside the world of others.

On the third morning that I was alive again, the girl whose voice I had heard the first night came in. I saw that she too had eyes shadowed by fear. She brought me a bowl of marrow broth and sat by me while I drank it. *He* was there, sitting on the bench opposite, stitching at a rawhide container, but paid no attention to us. She did not seem to fear him. Then she spoke, "You are better?"

Words I could understand! I smiled. "Yes." Then I asked, "Who are you? You speak almost like my people."

She nodded. "I am Bird. The Night People took me five winters ago. I was just a little girl, but I remember. I was from Tracker's *ahne*."

"Do you know what has become of my horse?"

"She grazes nearby in the sacred enclosure with White Horse, near the others. She is safe."

"The others?" Then I remembered that the Night People ate no other meat than horse, that they kept many horses for eating—and for another purpose.

"They have not hurt your horse or roasted her yet. They think she has magic because of her white marking and the way she comes to you."

My thoughts tumbled over one another. "She has much magic," I said. "Please tell them not to kill her, that she has *very much* magic." Bird nodded. Her eyes were quick and bright, like the little brown sparrows that come in flocks in the fall and rob our grain. There was a beauty like a softly shining light in her face, in spite of her fear.

The healer, as I thought of him, had been getting himself ready. Now he rose and, leaning heavily on his crutch, stumped out.

"Who is he?" I asked as soon as he was gone.

"He is your husband," Bird said simply.

For a moment I could not speak. I shifted myself painfully until I was almost sitting. "What do you mean? How can he be my husband?" I demanded.

Her mouth curved very slightly. "With the Night People, it is the custom for brothers or a cousin to give a bride to a young man. The Nameless One is without honor because of his foot. He was born that way. The Night People are not such kind people. His father would have had him killed, but his mother fought for him. He is very strong and can throw a spear well, but because of his foot he cannot be a hunter or have a name. His brothers thought it a great good joke to give him a dirt person as a bride. That is what they call our people. To them we are fit only to be slaves and worse. You are an injured dirt girl who, if she even lives, might not be useful. It was the greatest insult they could think of. They are still laughing. They have always treated him thus, except his father, who does not look at or speak to him."

"Do you have a husband?" I asked her.

She shook her head. "No. I am slave to the Nameless One's brother, Ice, and his wife, Shell." Her eyes slid sideways, as if she were hiding something from me.

"Do they hurt you?" I asked.

She stared at the fire. Then she nodded. "Sometimes he beds me instead of her, and she strikes me. She says that if I bear a child, she will kill both me and the child." She showed me her forearm with three red welts on it. "See. This is where she scratched me yesterday. But I am allowed to come and go. I care for their baby when she is tired of him." She looked at me. "I do not love them, but I love the child. He has not yet learned harshness."

"This Nameless One . . ." My voice trembled. "Will he hurt me?"

She shook her head. "I do not think so. At least I do not think he will beat you. He is not like the others. See how he has tended your dog—and you, even though to his people you are dirt. And he does not come with the others to watch the horses being butchered."

"How is it that my dog was not killed?" I asked.

"The Night People do not keep dogs for hunting as we do," Bird said, "but the brothers of your husband, who found you, admired your dog, who would defend you even though he was nearly dead himself. They allowed him to follow. The healer does not seem to care who or what he heals. It is simply what he does. His mother taught him. Now I think sometimes he teaches her. He makes medicine for her to ease the lump growing in her gut, but I think both of them know that some body evils cannot be cured. The others, even those who treat him as a dirt person, come to him for healing without shame—or thanks." Bird paused. Then she continued. "Earth Mother . . ." She said the words as if she had not spoken them for a long time. "Earth Mother has given him a great gift of healing. Most people with a wound like yours would have died."

I closed my eyes then in thanks to Earth, Sun, and the Spirit of Life, who had kept me alive and given the Nameless One the knowledge to heal me. Then I thought of another question. "Why does he not speak?"

She shrugged. "I do not know. I suppose he was born that way, too. But he hears," she said. "The old woman speaks to him, and he hears what she says."

It was much to think about, this being a worthless wife to a man with no honor or name. As I grew stronger, I watched for any sign of kindness from him. If his eyes met mine, they turned away. They were eyes that looked at far distances as he sat alone, brooding, but seemed to fly inward in the presence of others. I felt a small burning of jealousy when Bark left me now for short times, to follow at his heels.

Bird came often to see me, for she was eager to know if I knew her family and to hear about mine. I did not recognize the names she told me. I did not know there could be so many people in the world, but they must have come from another *b'ahut* that I had never heard of. Sometimes Bird brought the little son of Ice and Shell. He was big eyed and laughed easily, but he also showed signs of a fiery temper. Bird was hard put to keep him from pulling Bark's tail or falling into the fire pit and burning himself. But I could see why she loved him. Watching and holding him made me ache for Little Brother and Little Spring.

Bird helped me to walk outside for the first time. I sat by the doorway, breathing the sweet grass-scented air. How good the sun felt on my face! The hole in my shoulder was slowly filling with flesh again. The place would be ugly. I had seen scars from darts and spears before. My hand was beginning to work, but it was still an agony to lift my arm. I did not think it would ever be the same.

Bark was better too. He had learned to turn his head so that his one eye could see both ways, and he did not stumble so much. He came to sit beside me now, and I drew him to me, stroking the soft fur under his ears, kissing his muzzle. He looked at me with his one remaining eye. It was beautiful—a brown, shining ball with a black center, so deep it seemed to lead straight to his spirit. How was it that his one remaining eye was able to hold as much love as the two had done before?

I stared around me at the *b'ahut* of the Night People. It was much like ours, a haphazard cluster of pit houses with a haze of blue smoke above it, but over the entryway of every house were horse skulls in varying stages of decay. Some were still covered with tattered bits of flesh and hide. Others had been stripped by wind, rain, and sun to gleaming white bone. Still others had turned mossy and green, with jaws awry and teeth missing. All of them stared with great hollow eye sockets. I shuddered. So many dead horses.

I looked long at the herd of horses grazing beside the *b'ahut*. These people did not travel and camp during the summer. They ate one meat only, and that was horse. A longing for my home came so sharply that I had to close my eyes. How wonderful someday to have a whole herd of horses, not for meat, but as useful, hardworking friends grazing nearby! It was a dream that I thought now would never be.

I watched women working skins and stitching garments as they sat together outside their houses. The only difference here was that nearly all the skins they worked were horse skins. Children ran about, the little ones naked, shrieking and playing as they did at home. Then I noticed that there were no dogs anywhere to be seen, except for Bark, who lay by my side. I supposed that wolves and wild dogs still crept close at night to gnaw bones from the refuse pits, but there were no dogs lazing around the edge of the *b'ahut* in the sunshine, waiting to follow a hunting party. There were no puppies tumbling about the mouth of a nearby den or boldly scampering after a gang of screeching children. That seemed very strange.

In a meadow that lay between the curve of the river and the *b'ahut* lived the captured horses. I watched a young mare about Thunder's age. She grazed awhile, then took a step forward. As she moved, I saw something that made my heart cry out. The tendons of the little mare's hind legs had been cut, so she hobbled painfully on the first joints above the hoof. I wanted to be sick. With the curved arm of the river on one side and the *b'ahut* on the other, the Night People needed no fences. These crippled horses were nothing more than walking carcasses, waiting to have their throats slit. I struggled to my feet, tears streaming down my face. "Where is Thunder?"

"Look!" said Bird, turning me so that I could see a long pole with a pure white horsehide hung over the end of it, head, hooves, and tail still attached. It was set into the ground at an angle before a high enclosure of saplings. The sun gleamed on the whiteness of the hide, and the wind played with the ivory threads of the tail, so it looked like a horse of cloud or snow galloping against the blueness of the sky.

Inside the fence was another horse, and this one was a living horse, and he, too, was white. He was the color of moonlight on the winter steppe. Even from where I was, I could see that he was a beautiful horse, strong of shoulder and straight of leg, who lifted his head to the wind with the pride of an eagle. Beside him was a sand-colored horse. Thunder. Then she took a few steps and I saw, with a rush of relief, that she had not been mutilated. She looked happy beside this strange horse.

"White Horse is their god," Bird whispered to me. "The form of his father hangs above him. When he grows old, they will seek another white horse to replace him. Your horse is dun colored like all other horses, but the white mark seems to means something to them. They think she has been touched by White Horse, who is the creator."

"What do they do with White Horse?"

"They worship him. They sacrifice other horses to him."

I shivered. "How can they insult Earth Mother so, to waste the gift of food—of life?" My stomach turned inside me. Then I asked, "How is it that they have so many horses?" I counted nearly three tens.

"I think there are more horses in this country than ours," answered Bird. "Here I do not see many bison or other animals. They have a way of hunting the horses. There is a place where the river once cut through where the earth makes two walls that come together. They wait until a herd is grazing near there and the wind is right. Then they set grass fires, cutting off their escape, and chase them until they are trapped. They catch them with long poles with loops attached to the ends. It takes many men to drag one back. The horrible part is slashing their tendons."

I would have gone to see my horse then, but Bird held me back. "They will not like it. Ice says you are a witch who tries to gain power over the horse. I think it would be dangerous for you. Besides, you are tired," said Bird. "Come inside and rest."

Chapter Twenty-Two

Nameless

More than two moon cycles had passed since I was wounded. It had been early spring then. Now it was nearly summer. As soon as I could walk steadily, I crept out in the dark to see Thunder. The Nameless One slept soundly in his bed with his face to the wall. I was glad there were no *b'ahut* dogs around to signal that a person was walking in among the horses in the night. Bark came with me but knew enough to keep quiet.

The enclosure had been built strongly and high enough so that White Horse could not escape by leaping over. I slipped between the railings. Thunder was glad to see me. She tried to rub her face against my arm, telling me that she had not had a good scratch in a long time.

"No, Thunder," I whispered, pushing her away. "My shoulder is hurt." I rubbed her forehead and ears with my hand instead. Her winter fur was coming off in mats. Usually I helped her with shedding by combing out the loose hair. I had taken joy in working away the dull, shaggy winter hair until at last she wore her bright, smooth coat of summer. Now with the fingers of my left hand, I combed her as best I could. I thought that I would carve a new horse comb and keep it hidden, but then I told myself that I would not need to do that. As soon as I was stronger, Thunder and I would run away. It would be easy, because these people did not know about riding.

After a time I turned to look more carefully at White Horse. I drew in my breath. Never before had I seen a horse that was white all over. It was as if he were a horse made of milk, or moonlight. As he walked toward me, his hide seemed to glow with a light of its own. He put his muzzle into my hands, and I remembered that he had been fed and tended as if he were a god, ever since his capture as a foal. Under the glistening white hair of his coat, his skin was black.

He nosed me quietly. I reached up and stroked his arching neck. He was taller by the width of my hand than Thunder. He was an older horse, but not so very old, I could see. If he had not been captured, he would still be leader of his own herd. Not only was his color beautiful, but so was his form. When I walked back toward the fence, he followed me like a dog, and suddenly I felt in my heart that he was like Thunder. He, too, was a horse who had learned to be a friend to people, and so he, too, could be ridden. After that, I crept out nearly every night to visit both Thunder and White Horse.

Thus far I had managed to dress myself and eat with my left hand. Now I began to be able to hold a few things with my right, but I still could not lift anything or raise my arm. It was painful to let it hang by my side, so I kept it tied up in a sling. One day I found a good clump of reeds by the river. Slowly, with my one good hand, I pulled enough to make a small basket and carried them back to the pit house. I wanted to be useful, but it was difficult weaving with my left hand. My right was good only for holding the work steady. I nearly cried with frustration. After a time I looked up to see the healer person watching me. His face was expressionless.

Then he came toward me, put his hands to my shirt, and began to unfasten it. I shrank back, trembling, thinking that now I was stronger, the time had come and he would take me truly as his wife, but he shook his head. It was not my woman's body that he wanted. He only wanted to see my shoulder. He pulled open my shirt and traced his fingers lightly over the scars. Then carefully he began to knead the muscles around the wound. They were as tight and shrunken as dried rawhide. I had seen bone fragments in the bloody fluid that drained from the hole. My shoulder blade must have been shattered, for when I tried with my left hand to feel the place where the dart had entered my body, it felt hard, as if bone had been broken and knit back together again.

Gradually he worked the muscles with his fingers until I could not bear it and cried out. Then he lifted my arm and tried to move it slowly in a circle. I held my breath against the pain and tears ran down my cheeks. He shook his head at me. He put his hands on his own chest and took deep slow breaths. Then he nodded toward me, for me to do the same. While I breathed and the tears ran, he moved my arm. When he was finished, he simply turned away from me and began roasting a marmot that he had killed that morning.

After that, several times a day he made me move my arm. He made me press against his fist, which was like a rock, breathing with the pain, trembling with weakness.

Then after a time he gave me a grinding stone and motioned for me to grind barley. I thought, *He wants to make me fit for work.* He put firewood into my arms and motioned that I should carry it. Gradually strength came back to my shoulder, and it was not so painful to move. I was grateful to him. I did not fear him now, and began to hope that I could at least be useful.

One night after he had finished working my arm, he motioned for me to lift it and turn the shoulder by myself. I could do it—not well, but I could move my arm by myself.

He nodded.

It seemed strange to speak to someone who did not use speech himself or understand my language. Still, I whispered, "Thank you." He looked at me a moment, but I could not tell what he was thinking. I could not think that he felt anything for me, for I knew that to him I was a dirt person.

Inside my heart I ached for my family. I missed riding my horse. Bird was a friend, but still I was very lonely. I saw that my dog had accepted this man, and he had not hurt me, so I secretly watched the things he did, studying his face, hoping for some kindness from him.

His was not an ugly face, though hardly one to be called handsome, yet I found myself staring at it often. I began to like his somewhat overlarge nose and square jaw. I wondered how his mouth might look smiling, how his eyes, under their dark, straight brows, would look crinkled with joy. It seemed to be a face that knew little of happiness. Then I remembered how I had looked during the hungry time, and I thought that as sick as I had been, I must be ugly to him.

I was allowed to go to the river to fetch water, although I could still carry only one water skin at a time like a young girl. There was a gravel spit where clear, deep water could be reached easily without stirring up the gray clay of the riverbank. When the water bag was filled, I pinched off some of the clay and worked it between my fingers. It seemed like a good clay, and I decided that I would try to make something from it. I dug out as large a chunk as I could carry with my weak arm and took it back with me.

I had learned from Bird that there were several other captives in the *b'ahut*. Some had been taken young, so they remembered no other people or language. Others had grown old and no longer cared. They were allowed to come and go as they pleased, but they would always be considered slaves, never accepted as Night People.

Bird and the old mother had helped me take care of my body's needs. They had bathed me, washed the blood and dirt from my clothing, and mended the holes. Now it was good to be able to go to the river, scrub myself all over, and wash my hair. Bird gave me a comb. I dried my hair in the sun, gazing across the river and wondering how far it was to the sister river and then to my home river.

When my hair was dry, I combed it smooth and fastened it into a woman's knot. It was good to feel clean and to know that I smelled sweet again. I wondered if I might look nice to him, and I could not keep myself from glancing at him as I returned. But still the man who was supposed to be my husband did not look at me in the way that a man looks at a woman. Part of me was relieved. He was one of the Night People—I should fear him! But I did not fear him. Inside I still felt like a girl, yet another part of me felt something new that I could not understand.

Late that night I sat by the fire, working the beautiful gray clay on a flat stone. The clay from the banks of my home river was darker in color, almost reddish. This clay was white where it dried on the backs of my hands. I wondered what color it would be after hardening in the fire. Would it stay white? Would it hold its shape? Would I need to add ground mussel shells or some such thing to it to bind it together? I began shaping a simple cup and set my mind on running away.

I did not know the way home but thought it must be somewhere to the east, and anyway, all I needed to do was to ride Thunder and let her have her head. She had the horse's magic of knowing where home was. Secretly I would make a rope bridle. Thunder hardly needed anything more than a rope around her jaw. Badger had torn off her old bridle, and the Night People had not seen me riding her. They did not know that if I could get to Thunder, I could fly away from them faster than they could chase after me on foot.

But if I were caught, I might be killed. My heart shivered with fear at the thought of another spear in my body. Still, I think I would have had the courage to try to get to my horse in the night and run away, but something was holding me back.

I glanced over to where the Nameless One lay on his bed. As always, he lay with his face to the wall, but something about his back made me think he was not asleep. There was a stiffness about his shoulders, and I heard no steady, deep breathing.

I had a small wooden bowl full of water for working the clay. Now I held it so that the firelight playing on my face reflected on the surface of the water. Was I so very ugly? My eyes were like two pools of night with stars shining in them. I could make out the shape of my hair. It gleamed in the firelight too. My nose was not crooked. My mouth looked like a mouth—maybe the lips were too full, but it was not so very big. I pulled my lips back in a smile so that I could see my teeth. Except for the two middle ones on the bottom that turned a little toward each other, they were straight enough. There was a worn place on the bottom edge of one of my top teeth from cutting sinew, but I was lucky—there were no gaps. Then I noticed how foolish I looked smiling with my lips drawn back and I giggled.

The Nameless One moved restlessly, but he did not turn to see what was so funny. Crossly I worked again at my cup, and then suddenly the walls of it were too thin and it collapsed in my hands. I punched it back into a heap and closed my eyes, trying to squeeze back tears. Why did he not notice me?

In the end I took a handful of clay and made it into White Horse. I wished Little Brother were there so that I could give it to him, but that only made more tears come. Finally I wrapped the rest of the clay in a damp piece of leather and placed it in the corner. Leaving my little White Horse on the flat stone to dry, I took the goose-wing broom and swept the dried crumbs of my pottery making into the fire. Then I went to my own bed and I, too, turned my face to the wall.

I opened my eyes the next morning to see the Nameless One squatting by the hearth examining my handiwork. Perhaps he thought it was a gift. Very carefully, as if it were something precious, he placed it in the high niche above his sleeping bench.

The first time I witnessed the full moon ritual, Thunder grazed safely in the enclosure beside White Horse, in the cool light of the round Moon Child's face. The Night People gathered at a great central fire in the middle of the *b'ahut* before the form of White Horse's father. Several people beat upon round rawhide drums with the heels of their hands. Others shrilled on bone flutes or wailed an ugly song that sounded like keening for the dead and shouting joy at the same time. Knives and axes for the butchering were laid out in four places around the fire, a killing station for each direction that the wind blew. Four horses were selected and dragged, stumbling, up the pathway from the meadow toward the fire. In the light of the fire the horses' eyes rolled, flashing red with fear.

I stood beside Bird. The healer had not come out to watch. I said to myself that it was a cowardly way for people to get meat, but at least it was quick. When the blood was let from their throats, it was as if the horses suddenly grew weary. One by one they sank, first to their knees and then onto their sides on the ground.

When that was done, a fifth horse was led out. It had been kept in a tent entirely made of felted horsehair that stood a short distance from the sacred enclosure of White Horse. Bird had told me that the Night People believed the horse to be sacrificed must be purified by darkness. Earlier this one, the finest of the horses, had been confined there to be cleansed. Now she was led before White Horse. She was a big-boned, soft-eyed mare that came so quietly, I wondered if she, too, might be willing to carry a rider. Was there a race of kind horses in this strange country, and were these foolish people too blind to make better use of them than in wasteful killing?

A wizened old man held up a long, beautifully knapped blade of some foreign green stone. Bird whispered what he was saying.

"White Horse, Lord of the World, who has given us the brown horse for our food, we offer food to you." The blade flashed once on each side of the mare's neck. She snorted and stepped back a pace but beyond that hardly seemed to feel the sharp flint blade. When she was dead, wood was piled around her body and set alight. So much waste, the fuel and the flesh! It was an abomination to

Earth Mother. I turned my head away, sickened.

When Bark and I returned to the pit house, the healer was already sleeping on his bed on the far side of the hearth. Bark went over to him, sniffed at him, wagging his tail, then curled up on the floor beside my sleeping place. I lay awake in the night for many long thoughts. What did I feel for this cold man who had healed me but showed me no friendship? Why did I not just slip off in the night to my horse and ride toward the east until I found my people? Was Thunder really safe from the sacrificial blade? I finally slept.

He galloped astride White Horse, over the wide, rolling world of sweet grasses, under the blueness of the sky and the brightness of Sun Father. His mouth was partly open, showing strong, white teeth. There was a look of rapture on his face that made him beautiful. The muscles of his shoulders swelled: brown, hard, shining. Darts and spear thrower were slung over his back. He was a hunter of the Earth People, a skilled healer, with full honor. A name came into my mind: Owl.

I opened my eyes again in the darkness. To be one who rides the horse, the Spirit of the Wind, would give the

Nameless One a new life, as he had given me mine. I knew then why I could not leave.

"Bird," I said the next morning, "you must help me talk to the Nameless One who is my husband." So while he sat by the hearth, crushing the ingredients for a salve to ease the stiff knees of an old woman, I spoke to him in the few words of Night language I had picked up, with Bird filling in the gaps.

"There is a way that you could run over the ground faster than any Night hunter," I told him.

He glanced up at me, grunted in disgust, and went back to his work.

"Truly," I said, "the Spirit of Life has given us the horse for more than just meat."

"I do not think he will listen to you," Bird said to me in a low voice. "To him the Spirit of Life *is* White Horse."

"You have to tell him this," I said. "It is important. Tell him that a person can be carried on the back of a horse, run with the horse, like the wind that blows forever over the land. From the back of a horse it would not matter that he has no foot. The horse would be his feet, swifter than any man can run. He could be a hunter, have honor, have a name. Not every horse can be tamed, but some can, like my Thunder and her foal. I think his White Horse is such a one." Bird's eyes grew wide with fear. "Tell him!" I said.

When she had done so, the Nameless One flung down his grinding stone and looked at me with blazing eyes. He touched the place on his neck where an amulet would have rested if he had been allowed to wear one and angrily motioned something to Bird. Then he grabbed his crutch and, without bothering to lash on his wooden foot, hobbled outside.

"What is it?" I asked.

"He wants me to tell you the legend of White Horse. Then you will understand why you must not speak of sitting on the backs of horses."

She touched the little bone bird that hung around her neck. It was the storyteller's signal for beginning. "The Night People say that when the world began, it was winter. The land was white with snow. It rolled away in curves and dips like the back of a horse. It *was* the back of White Horse.

"Then White Horse snorted, and his nostrils were red with fire. The fire rolled out into the sky and became the sun, and the sparks from it the moon and stars. White Horse snorted again, and the breath steamed from his nostrils in clouds that became rain, rivers, and lakes.

"White Horse stamped a foot, and the fur of his back became the endless grasslands, green in spring, tawny in summer and fall, white in winter. He stamped another foot and all the other animals appeared. A third time he stamped, and First Man and First Woman appeared and stood with the other animals upon the immensity of White Horse's back looking out over the land. A final time White Horse stamped, and horses appeared, tawny as the late-summer grass, to run over the endless grasslands.

"Then White Horse said to Man, 'I give you the tawny horse for your food, but a horse that is the color of snow, like me, you shall worship and appease—for it is the image of the Master who created you.'"

I was silent for many thoughts, pondering what Bird had told me. I could understand how one might think it could be true, if that was all one knew. But I could not understand how anyone could not know how the warmth of Sun Father touches the richness of Earth Mother to create the Spirit of Life. How could he not know that Wind is the breath of this spirit and that the Spirit of Horse, Hekwos, was born of the wind? Hekwos runs over the endless grasses so that we can see and know that the Spirit of Life does not die, but runs forever with the wind that blows over the earth. I felt sad that the Nameless One did not know these things, but I knew in my heart, more surely than ever, that Thunder and White Horse, too, were gifts from the Spirit.

"The horse that is marked with white carries me," I told Bird, "but I am not her master—I am her leader. I have watched horses, and it is their way to have a leader. I do not beat or frighten her like a slave. I ride her because she allows it. I believe it is her joy to work for me as long as I ask no more than she can do. I believe that like the dog, she is a gift to us from the Spirit. Together, when I am on her back, Thunder and I become something different from what each of us was alone."

Then I told Bird of how I rescued Thunder and tamed her, how not only did I ride her, but how she dragged heavy loads for me and helped with hunting.

Her eyes grew wide. I am not sure she really believed me. After a bit she pressed her hand against my mouth, as if to stop my words, and looked over her shoulder fearfully in case the Nameless One had come back. "You must say no more, Fern. To the Night People White Horse is the Creator, the Master. The tawny horse is given for food and sacrifice, but I think they would kill you for trying to be the Master and sitting upon the backs of horses."

Chapter Twenty-Three

Owl

I could not help it. Night after night, while these fearful people slept and dreamed their fierce dreams and the Nameless One slept with his face to the wall, dreaming I knew not what, I crept out to the horses. One night I found that my arm and shoulder would bear my weight. In spite of Bird's warning, before I realized what I was doing, I was astride Thunder's back. Oh, the joy of the night wind in my face! How long would it take to find my people again? We could go—now!

But my dream of seeing the Nameless One riding White Horse came before my eyes, as bright as when I first dreamed of Thunder rising out of the river of mud with me on her back, and I could not go. Instead, I crept back to my bed in the silent house and lay staring through the darkness toward the one who slept turned away from me.

"You must try it," I whispered to Bird as we helped scrape horsehides after the butchering at the next full moon. "Thunder is strong enough to carry us both. The one who has no name could ride away with us on White Horse and become an Earth Person. The Night People have little love for him."

She listened, her quick brown eyes fearful yet sparkling, until one night she slipped away from the hearth of Ice and Shell and came out to the horses with me.

At first I taught Bird to ride within the enclosure. As the moon waned and the nights grew darker, we grew bolder and quietly unfastened the gate and brought Thunder into the meadow. It was full summer now, and the dark was like soft water. Soon Bird learned to sit through Thunder's bumpy trotting into the smooth flow of her canter. One night my friend slid lightly to the ground with a quiet laugh of triumph, flung her arms around Thunder's neck, and kissed her on the nose. "Thank you for such joy, *tisat* one!" she whispered.

"My turn now!" I whispered. Bird stepped back to watch, and I threw myself onto Thunder's back. My little horse flung her head up and, almost without being asked, galloped across the meadow to the river's bend and back. She slowed to a dancing trot, then stopped, inhaling the sweetness of the summer night with wide nostrils. I opened my arms to the sky and let my head drop back on my shoulders. "Spirit of Life," I sang softly, "I thank you for the gift of this friend, this horse."

That is when I turned and saw the silhouette of a man at the top of the rise between the meadow and the *b'ahut*, watching us. My breath caught. Was everything over? My thoughts swam until I almost thought I heard shouts of fury as the sacrilege became known, pounding feet, the flicker and stink of horse-fat torches, the soft whisper of long knife blades drawn from leather sheaths, the first thuds of the drums. . . .

Then I saw that the person leaned on a crutch, and knew that it was the Nameless One who saw us. My dog, not considering him a danger, had greeted him silently. Now the Nameless One stood transfixed, staring at us. Bird took to her heels and vanished in the direction of Ice and Shell's pit house. I dismounted and faced him, holding the reins of Thunder's rope bridle.

My heart drummed so loudly in my chest, I thought he must hear it. Would he kill me? *Now!* I told myself, I should leap onto my horse and gallop away from the Night People, away from this strange man whom I did not understand.

But I did not do it. My eyes were locked with his.

He made his way slowly to me. As he came closer, I could hear that he breathed quickly, as if he too were afraid. "Sh-sh-show me." He closed his eyes as if in pain. "Ri-de," he stammered.

"You speak," I said, not believing.

"N-n-n-not since b-boy." He looked away, and I thought I saw tear water in his eyes. "Fffff-f-father hit. B-b-better . . . t-to nnnn-nn-not spppeak—except f-few words t-t-to m-mother."

It took me a moment to comprehend what he had said. Then I nodded. I understood. When his father beat this crippled, nameless son for stammering, it had been easier not to speak at all—to become silent. I wanted to touch his arm to show him that my heart felt sadness for him, but I did not dare. Now I could see that inside this hard-faced person who did not show feeling was something very fragile, like the thinnest flint, which could be shattered at a careless touch.

I showed him Thunder, how she was my friend. I

turned her loose and then whistled the call of the soaring eagle, and she galloped back to me. I showed him that it was not abomination to ride on her back, but the honor of friendship between two creatures made by the Spirit.

His hand shook when he first reached out to stroke her neck. I showed him how she loved to be scratched under her jaw. Thunder behaved like the goddess of horses. She bent her head to tell him that she would not be insulted if he were to ride on her back. I showed him how to grasp her mane and fling his leg over. It took him several tries. I think it was harder for him because the leg with no foot was not heavy enough to help lift him when he swung it. But his arms and shoulders were powerful, and he was soon able to do it.

It did not take him long to learn to ride her, for in spite of, or perhaps because of, his missing foot, he was very strong. Yet he had the gentleness of a healer, which Thunder listened to, just as my dog had. As I led Thunder across the horse meadow in the secret dark of that first night, I looked back at the Nameless One, who rode upon her back. In the dimness of the starlight I could see that he was smiling.

After that my mind churned like a river after a storm. The next morning the Nameless One did not ask why I stayed when I could run away on my horse, but I knew he must be wondering. His eyes watched me, yet he did not speak. I knew that each time I went out to the horses in the night, I risked discovery. It would be foolishness not to go now, this moment—or the next. . . . Yet my stubborn heart told my brain that I would not leave before I had taught the Nameless One to ride.

That evening there were shouts, and we ran outside to see several men running toward our pit house carrying Snake, the oldest brother, to the Nameless One. He was the one with the bad teeth. Blood spurted from a wound the length of my hand on the inside of his thigh. The father, who was called Bull, came running behind, the old mother limping after him. Under his mask of tattoos the face of Bull was nearly as pale as that of his injured son.

"There was a fight," Tooth said, panting. "Fisher slashed him with his knife." The Nameless One was not listening. He had already snatched off his shirt and was pressing it against the wound. I knew the strength of his large hand, yet the blood continued to ooze through his fingers.

Snake's face was the bluish color of a freshly stripped hide. His eyes began to roll back in his head. Then the healer searched with his other hand for a place in Snake's groin, and pressed tightly there. The bleeding slowed and then stopped. I brought moss and clean wrappings. The healer showed me the place where he had made the bleeding stop, then nodded for me to put my fingers where his had been. While I held back the river of blood, he studied the wound. It was as neat as if Fisher had tried to slice meat instead of one of his own kind.

The Nameless One threaded a tiny needle with a long hair from a horse's tail and stitched the place where the blood had spurted from inside the wound. Then he threaded another piece of horsehair and stitched the edges of the wound together, leaving a gap for it to drain.

Snake groaned and had to be held steady all this while.

Finally the healer packed dried moss firmly against the wound and bound it in place with a long strip of soft leather. Then he nodded for me to let go.

All night we watched for the bleeding to start again, but the stitches and binding held. The leg did not swell and grow blue, so we knew that it did not bleed on the inside, either. In the morning Snake woke and was stronger. His brothers and father came and carried him to his own pit house. No word of thanks was spoken to the Nameless One, except that the mother put a hand on his arm and looked at him with tears in her eyes before she left.

When we were alone again, the Nameless One, who was my husband, lay back on his sleeping bench and put a forearm over his eyes, but I could see that he was weeping.

It was about this time that the Night People returned from a horse hunt empty-handed. It was the second time this had happened. The stock of horses in the meadow had dwindled. People began to murmur among themselves. Why was White Horse angry? Why did he withhold meat from his people?

Now the Nameless One spoke a few words to me when we were alone. He told me that his mother had a sickness which was eating her from the inside. She would not live much longer. He had told her, in halting words that brought tears to her eyes, about the horses, the joy of riding on a horse's back, and that here was his chance to be free of the hindrance of his missing foot. He told her that my horse was not insulted but shared the joy. I do not know what he told her about me.

She had seen how it was and told him to go away from his people. There was no reason for him to stay with those who would never acknowledge him even though he had been born one of them. He and his mother had already said their good-byes.

I thought that it was good I already knew how to talk without words to dogs and horses, because even though the Nameless One understood that I did not care how roughly the words broke and tangled as they came out of his mouth, he would never be one to speak many words.

In those secret nights, while I taught White Horse to carry me, Thunder taught the Nameless One how to ride. When I felt it was safe, we led White Horse out of his enclosure in the dead of night and let him run. At first he was so wild with joy, I nearly lost him. His enclosure had been only large enough for him to make short runs and sliding stops when the mares were in heat, or when the horror and stench of the ceremonial butchering panicked him.

Soon, however, he understood the language of the bridle and a rider's body. One night, when Moon Child was still small, like the curve of a bear's ear in the sky, we rode Thunder and White Horse in the meadow by the river, side by side. It was fearful, imagining what might happen if we were caught, but joyful to see this man, who had never moved over the earth without difficulty and pain, ride a horse. He threw back his head and laughed. It was as if the Spirit had given him wings. We stopped, and I turned to him in the dark. He sat upon

White Horse and there was a straightness in his back that had not been there before. I was still a little afraid of him.

"I know that I am only a dirt woman and a slave," I said, hesitating, "but in my dream you have a name. It is Owl—the silent one who rides the wind in the dark of night."

He stared at me, his face in shadow. I could not see his eyes. Then he nodded. After we let the horses back into their enclosure, he turned to me. "T-t-to-mmm-morrow we ggg-go."

He said that he would help me get back to my people. We decided that we would take Bird with us, if she wanted to come. The next morning I went to find her, to try to pull her aside so I could tell her. Bark was asleep in the sunshine. He did not hear me go. I think perhaps the blow from Badger's axe had damaged his hearing as well.

At this time of year the pit house doors were open to let in the fresh air, and often a family cooked at an outdoor hearth in front of the doorway. No one was there except Ice himself. He was hunkered over the stewpot, skewering out chunks of meat with his knife into a bowl. I had heard about this bowl from Bird. It had been fashioned from the top of a human skull. It was oval in shape, beautifully smoothed and fragile-looking in his big, hard hands. Seeing it now made the hairs on the back of my neck prickle. As I watched, he chewed slowly, with fat dripping down his chin, and then licked the drippings from the edge of the skull. There was no sign of Bird or his wife, Shell. Perhaps they were gone with some of the others, picking crowberries. I turned to go.

"You want Bird?" His words were slow and lazy.

"Yes."

"In there." He gestured toward the house. I stepped through the doorway, but Bird did not answer when I said her name. A moment later the hide door covering dropped down behind me, and in the blackness I felt Ice's hands on me, one around my waist and the other tightly over my mouth so that I could make no sound. I tried to bite his fingers, but he managed to keep them from between my teeth. I fought him, but he held me like a squirming puppy.

At that instant the door covering was ripped open again, and Ice was jerked backward.

He let go of me with a grunt of anger and turned toward his assailant. It was Owl. He pulled Ice back outside and slammed his fist twice into his jaw. I ran to the fire and snatched up a rock from the hearth. I was not afraid now. I burned with rage.

I did not need to use my rock. Ice lay stunned, with

two teeth broken and blood streaming from his nose. Owl took my arm and led me back to his pit house. I heard Shell's voice now, shrieking after us, "I will kill that dirt slave myself!" I turned to look back. The eyes of Ice looked after us with the hate of some kind of beast, but it was Shell's eyes that took away my breath. Her eyes glittered with a madness that was far more dangerous.

Bird had been looking for me. When she came to our house, saying Shell had gone to visit her friend, Owl had guessed I might find Ice alone and had come after me. Now he jerked his head eastward and said, "N-not www-ait."

We went into the pit house and I told Bird that we were going to take Thunder and White Horse and go. "We were going to leave tonight," I said, "but Owl thinks we should not wait. I went to find you, and Ice tried to— He grabbed me inside their pit house. Owl hit him and broke his teeth. Ice and Shell are very angry."

"Owl?"

"He is no longer the Nameless One. His name is Owl."

Bird's eyes grew big, and she smiled a little fearfully. "I think maybe that is a good name. But Fern, it is bad that Shell is angry. She had a first baby, before the one she has now, only it was female and it was stillborn.

There was a knot in the cord. There was nothing the Nameless One—I mean Owl—there was nothing he could do. Shell blamed him. She snarled like a beast and said he was a witch and not a healer, that he had caused her baby to die. But then Ice came and said Owl was to be thanked, for he would not have his firstborn a female. Shell was silent then, but I think she still bears a hatred for Owl." Bird continued, "She is very dangerous. She is beloved of her father, Elk, and many listen when he speaks."

"Thunder can carry both of us," I told her. "Will you come?"

"If we are captured, I think we will be killed," said Bird. "But the horses are fast. Yes, I will come with you."

"Do not go back for anything," I said.

I took down our two water skins. I had filled them earlier. Now I untied their necks and emptied them into the fire pit. "Go to the river," I said, handing them to Bird, "as if you were fetching water. If no one sees you, wade across and hide in the willow thicket on the other side. Two of us will not attract as much attention as three when we go to the horses, and if Owl and I fail to get away, no one will suspect you were part of this. Go now. We will look for you there."

Owl put an axe, several flint blades, and some dried

meat into the bottom of his healer's bag and slung it over his shoulder. I started to roll up a small sleeping fur. He shook his head at me and placed a berry basket in my hands instead. I understood. I was to walk out as if I were going berry picking and circle back to the horse enclosure when no one was looking. He would go a different direction—pretending to be on his way to tend a sick person—and meet me there.

Chapter Twenty-Four

Darkness

We had not gone six paces when we were stopped by a group of men, Owl's brothers and four or five others. They stood together like a wall of tall trees, blocking our way. Shell stood behind them. Tooth and Ice took me by the arms. Bark growled a warning rumble deep in his throat. Owl's knuckles showed white under the flesh as he gripped the strap of his healing bag.

"Nameless One," Tooth said to him, "White Horse is angry. We have allowed this dirt person in our *b'ahut*. Her horse is no god. This girl is a witch and has marked it with white to make us believe that. She is trying to destroy us. White Horse will give us no more horses for meat unless we kill the witch and her horse!"

Then Shell stepped forward. She had a mocking expression on her face. Her lip curled. "Nameless One, you have lived with the dirt person as your slave and wife. You tell us, is she a witch?"

There was a long silence that seemed to stretch into eternity while Owl's eyes were fixed on hers. Then slowly he nodded his head. Shell smiled with satisfaction.

I could not believe it. There was a feeling within me that was worse than knowing I was to die. I tried to make Owl meet my eyes. When he finally did, I thought there was a huge sadness in them. He shook his head very slightly. What was that supposed to mean? Ice and Tooth started pulling me away toward the purification tent near the killing place. Bark tried to follow, but Owl grabbed him by the scruff of his neck and held him back.

It was black and stifling inside the tent. My hands were bound behind my back, but the tent was pegged so securely to the ground, I could not have pulled up the edge to make a space to crawl under even with both hands free. I felt around and found the doorway fastened tightly closed. The darkness was like a smothering thing. I thought that this must almost be what it would be like to be buried under the ground. Why had Owl not fought for me? Why had he said I was a witch and let me be taken?

Soon I heard noises. The doorway was opened. Thunder was led in. The Night men said nothing to me, lashing the door flap down again. I knew that they would be guarding it on the other side.

In the darkness Thunder smelled me and nickered. I found her and pressed my face against her neck. She sniffed me carefully, looking for treats, then bumped me with her head as if asking why I did not at least pat her or rub her itchy places. She moved around, carefully smelling every corner of this sightless place. She whickered to White Horse in his enclosure, and he answered.

"Hush, sweet one, nothing will hurt you," I lied. I could not bear for her to be afraid. My beautiful Thunder, so willing, so good, so full of the Spirit of Life. How could anyone want to hurt her? I tried not to let my mind make pictures of my horse being led out, the long knife flashing, Thunder on her knees, dying. Then, I supposed, they would do the same to me. . . .

Terror seized me so that I could not move. I tried to think. My brain was frozen. Finally dull, slow thoughts began to swim in it, like fish under the ice of winter. Moon Child was only one quarter grown. Maybe they would wait until she was full. Yes! They always waited until the full moon for the killing ceremonies. But then I remembered that they did not have meat horses enough to last through the next moon cycle beyond that. If they thought the hunting was bad because White Horse was angry, they would try to appease him now.

After a time Thunder lay down, and I sat beside her and poured my tear water into the soft fur of her shoulder. She bore my foolishness like a patient mother.

Finally I stopped crying, stared into the darkness, and thought, *What would Grandmother do?* She would say I had wasted enough time with childishness. Weeping was not going to help us escape. Darkness was no reason to give up.

I forced myself to think. I wriggled around on my knees and bottom, searching the ground for some sharp stone to rub against the thongs that bound my wrists. Nothing. The floor of the tent was worn smooth by the feet of many horses. Sometimes I would feel a scattering of dried dung, but no sharp stones anywhere.

Over and over I thought, *Why did Owl let this happen?* He could have tried to speak, to fight, tried at least somehow to defend me. I had thought we had come to a friendship. There were feelings in my heart for him that I thought perhaps he was beginning to feel for me. Maybe he, too, believed I was a witch and had made the horse herds disappear.

But no, I told myself, he knew that White Horse was not unhappy, that he had taken Thunder for a mate and was pleased to be ridden and allowed to gallop in the night.

Then I thought about Shell and her smile as she asked Owl if I was a witch. What if he had said no? What would she have done then? The thought came into my brain as clear as a voice: *She would have said that I had bewitched him as well.* Then he, too, would be tied up in this tent, awaiting the night's killing, powerless to help me. There would not have been a way to win with Shell. I decided that I would believe that Owl was going to try to free me and that I would do my best to be ready. But what could one crippled man do against so many?

Thunder was still lying down. I realized that once she stood up again, there would be no way for me to get myself onto her. She stirred restlessly. Quickly I found her side and slid my leg over her back, just as I had so long ago when she was trapped in the bog—only this time she scrambled to her feet.

She must have been wondering how I was planning to ride her in this small, black place. I felt her shake her head up and down with impatience. Whatever it was I wanted—she was willing. When the door of the tent opened, whether Owl was waiting to help me or not, I would be ready.

So much time passed that I nearly lay down on Thunder's neck and slept. The thongs around my wrists cut tightly into the flesh. I kept wiggling my fingers, fighting numbness. I began to think perhaps the sacrifice would not be tonight after all.

Then at last I heard voices, a procession of Night People coming toward the killing place. Rawhide drums. The Song of Death. My heart thudded in my chest like a hammer stone against dead wood. I did not know if I could ride and keep my balance with my hands tied behind me. I leaned forward and took a clump of Thunder's mane in my teeth.

Thunder heard the drums and tensed.

Where was the doorway? I tried to judge by the sounds outside. I must be ready! There was a long pause in which I knew they would be setting torches to the great fire.

I was like a hare, quivering, hearing the panting, whining dogs, waiting to bolt from the brush when they closed in for the kill. My eyes searched the dark for a crack of light, some clue, but all was as dark as Grandmother's world.

More voices, a rustle, and the sound of the door flap

being unfastened. Suddenly, a little to my right, a triangle of flaming light and the black shapes of Night men. With the weight of my body I turned Thunder toward the light and beat my heels into her sides. She leaped over the Night men who had come for us, knocking them to the ground, scattering them like ashes before a storm wind. She bolted a few paces; then, perhaps blinded by the great fire or terrified by so many people gathered in one spot, she stopped.

Over the sound of people gasping I heard a shrill sound: the whistle of an eagle riding a keen west wind. It was the signal I had so often used to call my horse. It pierced the night, but it did not come from my lips. There was a murmur, shouts, heads turning, people pointing.

I looked where all eyes gazed.

Illuminated by the fire, like a vision in a trance, was a figure astride White Horse. His naked chest, arms, face gleamed an unearthly white, as white as the hide of the stallion. His eyes seemed to glitter. Beneath him White Horse snorted, his nostrils glowing huge and red. The stallion struck the ground with a forefoot, then half reared, sending people sprawling on their bellies and backsides.

The rider rode the plunging of White Horse like an

eagle rides the wind, and though I hardly recognized him, I knew this strange, shining apparition was Owl! He raised one arm in a gesture of command, and for a moment he *was* the God of White Horse. There was a rawness and power of horse and rider together as fearful as the specter of a whirling white blizzard or some black cloud shooting skyfire spears from its booming throat. The Night People cowered, faces in the dirt, mumbling and mewling in terror.

He whistled again, and Thunder galloped toward him. I saw then that he had his throwing stick and darts ready, but there was no need. People had fallen to their knees or lay prostrate on the ground. They were seeing what none of them had ever imagined—humans riding on the backs of horses. Were we witches or demons? Were we gods?

Owl saw that my hands were still tied behind my back. When Thunder pounded up beside White Horse, he held his knife out and slashed the thongs about my wrists. "Go!" he shouted, and there was no stumbling as the word came out.

I threw my weight toward the river, the east, toward home, and my little horse turned and raced away, with White Horse close behind her. Somewhere behind us, my dog barked loudly.

I turned my head then to see Ice, not ten paces to the side, spear thrower raised, taking aim at my heart. I knew a moment of stillness in which I thought I was dead. Then there was a scream as Ice jerked backward. His throwing stick was flung up over his head, the dart thrown awry, and he fell backward with a spear in his chest.

I turned my head again and saw in the shadows beyond the fire the form of another man on the back of a third horse. I would have believed they, too, were gods, except that I saw it was a small horse, one not yet fully grown. Beside them was a dog—my dog. I knew then that the Spirit of Life must be very near, for the man who had killed Ice before he could fling his spear to kill me, who had been warned by the frantic barking of my dog, was—my brother.

Chapter Twenty-Five

CHOSEN

Owl and I, on our horses, crossed the river in a wildness of splashing, followed closely by Flint and Hunter. The Night People had been too stunned to react. Not one had come after us as yet. On the other side we found Bird. How had she known to wait so long? She was shaking with fear, but I reached out my hand, and she swung up behind me onto Thunder's back.

Now several Night men appeared on the opposite riverbank, but we were out of range of their spears. We galloped until the horses were tired, allowing Thunder and Hunter to choose the direction, then walked to rest them, always moving toward where the sky was growing lighter.

When we had crossed the sister river, I halted Thunder and slid off her back, making Bird do the same. "She is tired," I said. "We must let the horses drink and rest a bit. The Night People cannot follow so fast on foot." Bark leaped from one to the other of us, crying like a puppy in his joy. Flint slid down from Hunter's back, and I threw myself into his arms. "Brother, is it really you?" I could feel him tremble as he held me.

"We are brother and sister," he answered. "I would hunt until I found you. After the rains, there were many days when we could not cross the river. When finally we did, there was no trail to follow. Hunter is still a baby, and often I was forced to walk beside her to let her rest. Still, Old Flint could not keep up with the horse, and after a time he had to go back."

Now I was laughing and crying at the same time. I punched him in the chest then and said, "What took you so long, you miserable brother of mine?" Then for a time I sniffled and sobbed while he explained to me.

"We found the body of Badger and believed he had been killed by Night People, but we did not know if you lived, and if you did, in what direction you had been taken. It is a very big world in which to hunt for one small, knows-all-things sister. If you cry any more, you will make the river flood again."

I wiped my eyes and splashed water on my face. We let the horses drink, but not enough to bloat their stomachs and sicken them.

Owl handed me the reins of White Horse. Then he hobbled to the river's edge, waded in below where the horses were drinking, and began washing away the white clay with which he had painted his body. When he came out of the river again in his brown skin, shaking the water from his hair, he was no longer the God of White Horse. He was just a crippled young man with a homely face.

Yet he had not abandoned me. He had been ready to fight all his people alone for a dirt slave. For that he would always look like a god in my eyes.

Bird drank and then sat quietly on a rock. I could see that she was tired. I patted Hunter, admiring how strong and hard she was for a horse only a year and a half old.

"Soon she will be as wise as your Thunder," my brother said proudly, letting her rub her face against his back and laughing when she nearly pushed him into the water. He nodded toward Owl. I could see that Flint had noticed Owl's lameness, but he said nothing. "Does he understand our tongue?" he asked under his breath.

I nodded. "The Night language is not very different from ours. It is how they say the words that is most different. It is deeper and sharper somehow. He has grown used to my speech. He was scorned by the Night People because of his leg, and because his tongue does not work well for speaking any language. To them he was the Nameless One, and always silent, but the Spirit has given him a great gift for healing. He gave me my life again when Badger put a dart through me. His name is Owl." I did not tell my brother then that to the Night People, Owl was also my husband.

Then Flint said to Owl, "Thank you for healing my sister—and for helping her escape." Owl nodded. Flint turned admiring eyes on White Horse, taking in the full, glimmering beauty of the stallion.

"He is the god of the Night People," I said. "I do not know what they will do now that he has been stolen from them. They believe that White Horse is the creator of everything. To them it is abomination to ride a horse. They believe he is our master, not our friend. But White Horse was not happy being a god. Like Thunder and Hunter, he is a horse that is willing to be ridden. It is his joy to run for Owl."

We walked knee-deep in the river for a time, leading the horses to rest their backs. It was difficult for Owl, even though he used White Horse's strong neck as a crutch. We hoped to make our trail harder to follow. The sky was bright gold to the east, and the stars had all gone out. "When did you find the *b'ahut* of the Night People?" I asked Flint.

"Two days ago," he answered, "but I was waiting for a chance to find you alone. When I saw Thunder in the enclosure with White Horse, I thought you might still live. Then this morning Bird came to the river by herself, and I thought for a moment it was you. When I saw she was not, I captured her, hoping she could tell me something."

Here I saw that their eyes met. Bird did not look unhappy about being captured by my brother, and I smiled. "She was taken by the Night People five winters ago from Earth People like us somewhere in the world," I told him. "She was a slave. She will be happy, I think, in our *ahne*."

It was nearly nighttime again when we at last came within sight of tents beside the river. We did not know if it was our own *ahne*, but at least it would be people of our *b'ahut* and they would be familiar to us. Dogs yapped and howled to signal our arrival. My dog tore off joyfully to greet them.

Then someone saw us and must have recognized Hunter and Thunder. In a moment others came running.

I saw a tall man shading his eyes with his hand against the sun's last rays, and I knew it was my father. It *was* our *ahne*! Then I saw my mother flying up the hill, carrying a squealing little child. Could that plump little thing be my baby—my sister—Spring? Finally a stooped figure with a stick made her way out of one of the tents. She stopped and looked toward where we were shouting and calling. Her wrinkled face split into a grin of delight.

"Grandmother!"

Thunder snorted and tugged at the reins. We were home.

I turned to tell Owl that this was my *ahne*, part of my *b'ahut*, my family. He had halted White Horse several paces behind us. I wheeled Thunder around and cantered back to see what could be the matter.

Owl was staring away at the endless grasses of the steppe. "I www-ill l-leave you hhh-here." He did not look at me. His face seemed to have turned into stone.

"But where would you go? My people will welcome you. You cannot live in the vastness of the world alone!" I felt like I was falling into darkness, a smothering blackness, like that of the purification tent.

"I h-h-have l-lived alone among mmm-my own ppp-people."

My heart tore inside me. "But you are my husband,"

I said almost in a whisper. "I thought we had a friendship."

He looked at me then, and the pain of a wounded animal was in his eyes. "Y-y-you h-had no ch-choice. I wwwould not t-take a woman who h-had n-no choice."

I nudged Thunder with my leg so that she moved close beside White Horse and reached for one of Owl's big hands. Then I looked into his eyes, to see the joy when it came into them at last, as I knew then that it would. "And what if it *is* her choice?"

Chapter Twenty-six

After

Many seasons have passed. Every spring Thunder has given our *ahne* another foal. Each one carries her friendly heart. Each is a new gift from the Spirit.

My brother's horse, Hunter, has also given us foals. The children of Hunter and White Horse are tamer than those fathered from the wild herds. But the kindest, most beautiful foals of all are the children of my Thunder and Owl's White Horse.

The horses of our *ahne* graze near us wherever we go, for we have also learned to breed dogs like Bark, who have hearts for guarding as well as hunting. Other *ahnes* have a few horses now, but we do not trade our tame horses cheaply. The sight of our horse friends grazing peacefully by our tents and pit houses, ready at any time to help us hunt or work, will ever be beautiful to me. I never tire of their presence or the wonder of riding them—especially my Thunder.

Often when she lies dozing in the soft grass on a summer morning, I stop my doings for a few moments to sit beside her. She twitches her ears at flies while I lean against her warm side, trusting me completely. I thank her for her strength, which she so willingly lends to us; for the joy of our friendship; for the pride her taming has given me—and most of all for my life, which she has saved many times over.

White Horse begins to grow old now. I know it grieves Owl, for White Horse is to him the freedom he could never know before with his crippled leg. White Horse has made him a respected hunter as well as a healer who travels far over the grasslands when summoned. White Horse has given him his very identity.

Often I see them speaking together, each in his wordless way, gazing into one another's eyes, as if they know that the time will come when the Spirit of Life must part them.

But there is a son of White Horse and Thunder, a milk-colored two-year-old! He shimmers like the air over the summer grasslands when he runs. He is not quite finished with his baby foolishness, yet he knows how to listen with his body as well as his ears, and he has a sweetness like meadow flowers or birdsong that sometimes brings tears to my eyes.

My body, too, has swelled with the Spirit of Life and given us our two babes, Twilight and Mist. My sister, Spring, now nearly six winters old, still tries to carry Twilight on her hip, like a big doll, though my older daughter is a strong child who can walk by herself perfectly well. The two of them are like sisters. They follow me about in my work as horse keeper for the *ahne* and believe themselves to be expert riders because Thunder is too kind and lazy to run away with them. Sometimes they spend a whole morning on Thunder's back, laughing and whispering together, or just dreaming as little girls do. Thunder is like their patient auntie, plodding carefully along at the urging of their small heels drumming against her sides, or grazing contentedly when her riders give her some peace. They are safe on her, under the tireless gaze of Watch, the blue-eyed daughter of my faithful old Bark.

Mist still spends much time napping in her sling on my back, but already she holds out her arms to her grandmother Moss, or squirms to go to the rough embrace of

Old Flint. She is wide-eyed like her sister, and just as beautiful and strong, though a better sleeper. If ever I should voice my fear that my husband might wish I had given him sons, Owl puts his fingers to my lips and shakes his head. Then his eyes turn to his two girls and I see the same softness in them that I see when he looks at me. "Th-they are perfect," he says.

I will not try to put into words the goodness of the man who is no longer the Nameless One but truly my husband, Owl. It will, I think, always be painful for him to talk with words. He has taught me that there are other ways of speaking. One has only to look into my eyes to know what I feel for him.

A small white owl with outstretched wings, carved from horse bone, hangs upon his chest now. It was my gift to him when he joined our *ahne*. Across his cheekbones are tattooed the footprints of a running horse, which he asked me to draw for him, rubbing ash into the needle pricks. I did not want to do it, but he laughed at the pain. I was afraid it would make him look fearful, like a Night man, but it did not. I have come to accept the marking on his face. It is part of who he is. He said it was something that he needed to do, that not all Night People are harsh, that perhaps someday we can teach them kinder ways. I hope he is right.

It is a wonder that Grandmother is still with us! Her seamed and weathered face makes the very rocks look young. Now that I am older, I see that we grow *inside* ourselves too, and that my little, wise, shriveled grandmother, whose real name is Seed, fulfilled her own Naming Day blessing better than anyone I ever knew. She has taken Owl under her wing, teaching him all her preparations and cures. Her blindness and his silence seem to complete each other, so between them there is nothing lacking.

Moss and I still do not understand each other's hearts in all things, and I know that I will not always have Grandmother, but my brother Flint's wife, Bird, has become as dear as a sister to me. Our Twilight and their Little Flint, born in the very same moon cycle, often put me in mind of my twin brother and me: now play-fighting each other like puppies, now fighting as one to pull a sturgeon from the river. But when Spring, Twilight, and Little Flint all together try to ride Thunder, she sometimes bounces the last child, whose weight is on her rump, with funny little bucks, until all three of them tumble, shrieking with laughter, into the grass.

Except for the loss of Bark—his poor old body now lies at the entrance of our pit house, which he guarded so long and well—Owl and I have not yet been touched with death. For that I am very thankful. But we are human, and grief must come to us sometime as surely as all the joy we have known. Still, the Spirit has given us strength to bear grief when it comes. And we have each other.

Just today Twilight and Little Flint came running to me. Spring and my old friend Berry's daughter, Fawn, were hand-in-hand behind them. They had been with the other children gathered for storytelling at Hawk's fire.

"Fern-Mother," said Twilight, her eyes glowing as if they were still filled with firelight, "Hawk told us the story of how horses came to be friends of our *ahne*! He said it was *you* who brought them, *you* who tamed the first one, which was Thunder!"

"Silly, I've told you all that before," I said, gathering them in my arms so that I was like a tree full of roosting birds, with giggling children climbing onto my back as well as my front. I winced a little at the pull on my old wound, but it was worth it.

"But I like to hear it from Hawk," she answered me. "It seems truer that way."

I smiled. I am often spoken of at the storyteller's fire these days. They have a name for me, *Wind Rider*, but I still use my old name, Fern. It was that which led me to

Thunder and to become who I am now, and it was given to me by my mother. When I was a child, we only watched horses run. Now we ride them, and a fierce joy fills my heart, for it was a young girl who gave us this gift of freedom and power, a girl who felt trapped by old and narrow paths. But then I think it does not really matter who was first to ride a horse, to fly with the Spirit of the Wind. What matters is that we have been given the gift of horses that all may ride.

They speak of me along with our healers, our strongest hunters, and our wisest old people, but that is no longer important. I have my loved ones, my dogs and horses, and the sweet, endless grassland. I am a wind rider. It is a thing that a woman can do as well as a man. That is more than enough.

ACKNOWLEDGMENTS

One might call *Wind Rider* a work of science fiction. Looking backward into prehistory is just as mysterious, enticing, and difficult as peering into the future. Without the written word there is only archaeological evidence and guesswork to go by. We fiction writers are charlatans who weave elaborate fabrications—but the truest fiction is based on fact. In searching for morsels of information that might make Fern's and Thunder's story more believable, I encountered some very generous people working in such specialized fields as anthropology, zooarchaeology, osteoarchaeology, and linguistic paleontology. Through their kindness and patience I was able to imagine the place and time where horses are thought to have been first domesticated: what is now Kazakhstan, six thousand years ago.

Busy researchers might be excused for ignoring an unknown writer's request for information, but time and again I found otherwise. Some of the premier researchers on ancient horses, Dr. David Anthony and Dorcas Brown (Hartwick College, Oneonta, New York), Dr. Marsha Levine (Cambridge University, U.K.), and Dr. Sandra Olsen (Carnegie Museum of Natural History, Pittsburgh) provided articles for me to read, answered questions, and directed me to even more researchers. Dr. Nerissa Russell (Cornell, Ithaca, New York) and Dr. Naomi Miller (University of Pennsylvania, Philadelphia) were both helpful. Dr. Linas Daughnora of the Lithuanian Veterinary Academy (Kaunas, Lithuania), Department of Anatomy and Histology, sent me his book. (Now I can return the favor!) Alan Outram (University of Exeter, U.K.), who has studied evidence of horse domestication through milk lipids on pottery shards, not only patiently answered questions but wrote lengthy descriptions that helped Fern's world come alive for me.

Dr. Martin Huld and Dr. Karlene Jones-Bley

(UCLA) and Richard Brown (U.S. Department of State) helped me to understand some of the intricacies of language. Because of difficulties with typesetting and reproduction of sounds, in the end I decided not to give my characters names from the Proto-Indo-European (PIE) language that was most likely spoken in that time and place; but certain words did work their way into my story, most notably *hekwos*, a PIE word for horse, and *kolki*, a Russian word still in use today to describe the patches of woodland that dot the steppe. Other words came from my imagination.

I am particularly indebted to Dr. Olga Potapova, collections curator of the Mammoth Site, Inc., Hot Springs, South Dakota, and an expert on ancient bird life. She shared with me that her family name is the sacred word for *bear* and still a common last name in Russia. From her research I found details such as the use of an owl's wing to fan away biting insects and the significance of the golden eagle—still the symbol on the state emblem of Kazakhstan. Dr. Potapova kindly read my manuscript and made suggestions, for which I am very grateful.

A big hug goes to my old friend Bob Berg (www.thunderbirdatlatl.com), who demonstrated the use and construction of his beautifully made spear throwers and darts, described the killing of a boar, and advised me at length on primitive life, hunting, and the problem of cross-dominance.

I'd like to thank Susan Stafford, an editor who some time ago published the embryonic beginnings of Fern's and Thunder's story in a little Canadian magazine called *Horsepower.*

One way to survive the struggle of becoming a writer is through the support of writers' groups. I am lucky enough to have several: the Pondhouse Writers of Alfred, New York; the Coudersport Pennsylvania Writers; the Rochester Area Children's Writers and Illustrators (RACWI); the Society of Children's Book Writers and Illustrators (SCBWI); and of course my dear old drawing group. I love and admire all of you. A special thank-you goes to the YA writer Mary Beth Miller, who called me straight from the shower one morning with the title for the book!

I thank my husband, wood artist Fred Beckhorn; daughters Fern and Spring, and the rest of my family, for their unwavering support; our dogs, Spike and Chloe, for guarding every step of mine that is in their power to guard; and my rugged little Morgan horse, Katie (who has been known to graze upon ripe timothy heads at a full gallop), for the joy of riding.

To those I have forgotten, please accept my apologies and thanks as well. All mistakes herein are my own.

And to my editors, Jill Santopolo and Laura Geringer, thank you both for believing in *Wind Rider*.

SUSAN WILLIAMS writes stories for young readers because "when I was a kid, books meant everything to me." She loves visiting schools and libraries to talk about writing and to run writers' workshops. Susan Williams lives with her husband, two daughters, and many pets in the wilds of western New York. You can visit her online at www.susanwilliamsbeckhorn.com.